LINCOLN'S LETTER

David S. Leonard

DAVID S. LEONARD

david.leonard478@gmail.com

541-280-6175 Oregon,
USA

LINCOLN'S LETTER

DAVID S. LEONARD

iUniverse, Inc.
Bloomington

Lincoln's Letter

iUniverse books may be ordered through booksellers or by contacting:

iUniverse
1663 Liberty Drive
Bloomington, IN 47403
www.iuniverse.com
1-800-Authors (1-800-288-4677)

ISBN: 978-1-4759-5275-9 (sc)
ISBN: 978-1-4759-5277-3 (hc)
ISBN: 978-1-4759-5276-6 (ebk)

Library of Congress Control Number: 2012918487

Printed in the United States of America

iUniverse rev. date: 10/09/2012

CHAPTER 1

Letters

D AVID WAS BUSY RUMMAGING IN the attic brushing cobwebs aside with the whisk broom. Where was that box? It might well contain a fortune in Civil War letters, stamps and memorabilia. It might even supply enough money so he'd not need to get a summer job! He quickly pushed the thought away. Oh, he might sell them to help with *college*. He'd be graduating from high school in a couple of weeks and finances were a worry.

He set aside an old box and wiped his forehead of the beads of sweat. It sure was hot up here. And he was sick of bumping his head on rafters. Then, a gleam caught his eye. It was something sticking out of the old, dusty insulation. The attic must have been built nearly a hundred years earlier he thought as he made his way to the thing just visible in the insulation. He pulled it out seeing what looked like an old helmet. A fascinating helmet . . .

Before leaving school that Friday afternoon he'd been asked at least three times what he planned to do this weekend. He wasn't sure and wasn't worried about it. That was half the fun . . . no bells, no time schedule and *no plans*. It would take care of itself.

Reaching home—a really old and large structure—before his Mom, he turned to the baseball game. It was totally out of reach for the Cubs. He turned it off and walked out to the front porch and sat on the porch swing. His best friend, Jake, was off somewhere with his dad getting supplies for the new ramp. They had to build it for Jake's mom. So Jake would be busy most of Saturday.

Without Jake around he'd just study more on Lincoln and the Civil War. Today, though, he felt a need to be with someone.

Maybe he'd go over to Aunt Gin's place. Still, he was torn. The mystery of the Confederate battle plans prior to the battle of Sharpsburg—"Antietam" in Yankee-land—fascinated him. The plans had been found on a Reb camping ground wrapped around three cigars. A clearly authentic copy had been delivered to the Union Commander. Why hadn't McClellan taken advantage of his incredibly good fortune? He hadn't. *Why*? David would die to know. It was his secret plan to pursue this mystery!

His Aunt Gin lived just down the street in a similar house. He ate a stale donut and decided to see her. She was his favorite of all his family. His dad lived upstate, so it was just his Mom, himself and his Aunt Gin . . . actually *Great*-aunt Gin. She had a full head of white hair—*thin* white hair. And, she was *tiny* with a wonderfully happy disposition. "Tiny" described her. "Small" was an inadequate description, David thought. And, she almost always had a wry smile. Somehow, she was fun to be around.

Her name was really Virginia, but, since earliest childhood, she had been *Gin* to David.

He knocked on the door, and walked in. Gin was watching her soap. He sat and watched. At the end, she turned it off and asked how the day had gone.

"Not bad."

"What are your plans?"

"Don't have any."

"How about your summer job?"

"Haven't found one, yet."

"Well, then, would you mind going up to the attic and looking for some stuff for me?"

"Sure. What you looking for?"

"Somewhere I have a bundle of letters written by my great-great-grandmother, Julia. Let's see, that would be three or four *greats* for you."

"Ah! The one who got the President Lincoln letter which you're giving me!" He grinned and hoped he might jar some new memory out of Gin.

"She was married to the Civil War soldier who was killed. He did something special, and President Lincoln wrote that letter to her. You know all this."

David was fanatic about the Civil War. He read everything he could get his hands on about the War *and* Abraham Lincoln. Abraham Lincoln had been America's greatest President, he thought. This was not the first he'd heard of the President Lincoln letter being sent to his great-great or greater-grandmother! And it was his! Well, it was his when he graduated in two weeks.

"Have you read the letter?"

"I think my grandmother read it to me when I was a little girl. Seemed to me there was something about *cigars* in it. But I can't remember what it was. It wasn't too short, as I recall. But, you'll read it yourself in two weeks!"

"Do you know what battle it was where he died?"

"It was a battle somewhere near Washington. I think it was in Maryland."

"Could it have been Antietam or Sharpsburg?"

"Why, I think it was called *Antietam*!"

"Is it still in the safe deposit box?" His heart was beating fast. *Antietam* and *cigars* and a Lincoln letter which *wasn't too short*! That was highly unusual for a Lincoln missive!

"Yes, but don't worry. I'll have it here when we cut your graduation cake!"

David had only found out about the letter a month before when Gin surprised him at his birthday saying she had a special gift for him when he graduated from high school.

David was amazed. How could anyone have a letter from *Abraham Lincoln* and not know what it said? Why wasn't it framed and hanging on the wall? Instead, it was in a safety deposit box! And how about . . . those letters up in the attic! *Civil War letters!*

"Where should I look?" It was hard to take his mind off the Lincoln letter. What a prize that might be if it addressed what he hoped it might!

"The last I remember they were in a flat wooden box . . . about the size of a case of soda. And, that's probably buried under a lot of other boxes and stuff. If you find them, I'll let you have some of the Civil War letters."

He almost ran up the creaking old stairs to the attic. Once, he'd looked in at it but turned away. It was dusty with lots of cobwebs and had only the one light bulb hanging down in the center of the dark room.

He opened the small door and stooped to enter. His tall six-foot frame would be a handicap in these quarters. He could just see the light bulb suspended on a cord from the center of the ceiling. It was as he'd remembered. He brushed the cobwebs aside and pulled the cord. The light failed to come on. Swatting at cobwebs, he retraced his way back to the small door.

Gin directed him to a closet in the kitchen where he selected a 100 watt bulb thinking he'd want as much light as possible. Then he thought of all the cobwebs he'd battled and looked for something with which to brush them away.

"Hey, Gin."

"Yeah?"

"where can I get something to knock down the cobwebs?"

There was a moment of silence as she thought. "There's a whisk broom on the floor by the refrigerator."

Picking up the small broom he went back up the stairs thinking it might be nice to have a flashlight. He changed the bulb and it gave a bright glow but failed to illuminate the dark places among the boxes, furniture and trunks. He briefly wondered if he might get one of the old windows open to get fresh air but knew he'd not even be able to get to a window without moving a ton of stuff.

He looked with dismay at the huge assortment of cardboard boxes, trunks, suitcases, old furniture and miscellaneous goods in the room. It was a large house, and the attic extended the lenth of the house which he estimated to be at least forty feet. And the width must have been thirty feet or more. Whew! Maybe he should go into the antique business.

Without much thought about where to begin, he started pushing and stacking furniture, open boxes of paint brushes and rollers, old books, old dishes, and junk into the center area which was already cluttered. This was going to be a job. The walls were lined with more boxes and furniture. The ceiling slanted down to two or three feet from the floor on each side. There were windows on each end of the long room but with so much dirt that little light came into the room. And, the bottom half of the windows was obscured by boxes and junk stacked on the floor.

He worked hard for at least two hours pushing and carrying boxes to the stack he'd started in the center area. At last he had an eight foot area cleared down the wall. But still no wooden box. He wiped his forehead. Then, he saw the gleam in the insulation.

It looked like an old helmet like ones he'd seen in his history books.

David turned the light off and made his way downstairs with helmet in hand.

"No luck, yet, Gin. But, what is this? Looks like an old helmet."

"Let's see." She peered closely at it and shook her head. "I have no idea. Never saw it before." After a pause, she said "Maybe it was left here by the old man who owned the house before me. You can have it."

Later, he would shake his head in wonder at how casual she had been.

David shrugged and carried it home.

"Hey, Mom," David yelled as soon as he got through the door.

"Yes?"

"Guess what Aunt Gin's giving me?"

"What?" she replied, and continued unpacking groceries.

"She's giving me some Civil War letters, if I can find them."

"She's already giving you that Abraham Lincoln letter. What's that in your hand?"

"Well, the letters are somewhere in her attic. If I can find them, she wants to give me some."

"Well, if you get something valuable, we may have to talk about it. And, there's the Lincoln letter. How much is that worth?" She turned to look at her son. He had her height, was actually taller at a good six feet, and was thin. He was handsome and quite mature, she thought.

"What's to talk about? She giving it to me."

"I understand, David, but that letter was written by *Abraham Lincoln*; it could be worth a lot of money. No, Aunt Virginia is nearly eighty-eight and needs to be made aware what she is giving away. I mean *aware of how much it is worth*. She is your great-aunt and may have need of money. We don't know how she may feel if you can get a large sum of money for the letter."

David couldn't imagine why someone of *that age* would need money for anything, but what the heck! He had no objection to sharing with Gin. He had no desire to sell *any* of the letters if he could find them. And, he's never sell the Lincoln Letter!

No one realized how he felt about the letter. Maybe they never would. His secret wish was to do extensive research and write about Lincoln's dealings with General McClellan.

Now, that letter might be of far more significance than he'd ever dreamed. He had to have it! The Lincoln letter he'd receive could be the start; he might launch himself into a search for the truth about some of the mysteries which surrounded McClellan and his relationship to his Commander-In-Chief. One of the greatest mysteries was that which surrounded the lost Confederate Battle Plans regarding the Battle at Sharpsburg.

But, he wasn't worried about Aunt Gin. She gave him money every Saturday to buy her groceries. She was not one to care about wealth. He knew Gin as no one else seemed too. And, she owned the old house, so how much money did she need?

"You look like you need to clean up for supper." And so ended the conversation about *letters*. He tossed the helmet on his bed before washing for supper.

CHAPTER 2

Discovery

D AVID WAS UP EARLY, FOUND a flashlight and a pair of Dad's old leather gloves and was ready for the day's work. After a fast bowl of cereal, he walked across to Gin's. Mom was sleeping-in but knew what his plans were, so he'd not be missed.

He started by looking around the entire attic for the wooden box. There was no sign of it, so he figured he'd no choice but follow the plan he had started. He put down a strip of black electrical tape on the floor out from the boxes on the left where he'd found the old helmet. His idea was to begin by moving the boxes and other items to the left from the stuff on the right. There was just no room left in the center.

The old helmet had him fascinated. It was beautiful. It seemed to be made of inlaid silver and gold. It was exquisite. David knew about cleaning antiques and carefully avoided rubbing dirt and grime off. He'd take it somewhere for an expert to examine it.

By Saturday evening he'd reached the windows at the end of the attic and figured he'd searched maybe a fifth of the stuff. He was beginning to wonder if there even was a wooden box. Or, maybe, he was just too tired.

Sunday, after church, he considered returning to the attic, but Jake had appeared and wanted to go fishing. It was just too tempting. Fly fishing was his newest passion. They would ride out to the river with Jake's uncle Bob, an inveterate fly fisher. His collection of flies was enormous. It was amazing what he'd pay for a fly. He even had one fly that had cost him more than a hundred bucks! Maybe he even had ones that cost more. He'd taught the boys how to cast dry flies and even how to do *roll* casts.

Evening brought them together at the truck each with an assortment of trout. Jake's uncle Bob released most of his fish but kept a couple for supper. After comparing their fishing episodes, they headed home. It was only then that David thought about the Civil War letters and excitedly told Jake and Bob. They expressed interest but not the excitement that David expected. Well, they'd get interested when he found them and had them appraised. He'd forgotten the helmet.

Bob was a short man of middle age with graying hair. His mustache was white. His blue eyes were intense above a perpetual smile. He liked Jake and David and loved to show them the intricacies of the cast and the mysteries of flies for each season. He laughed easily and found no fault in the boys. The trip home with Jake and his uncle was always a joy with funny stories and humorous episodes of the day's fishing.

It was too late for any work up in the attic, so David put his fish in the freezer and caught a quick shower. Then, he laid out his clothes for school, caught a late game on TV, and thought about the end of his senior year. It would come next week. Then, he'd have his Lincoln Letter.

The end of the school year always brought worry about what he'd be doing during summer. Last summer he'd worked with Jake's uncle Bob planting trees and shrubs. It had been good work, and he'd enjoyed it except for the really hot days. He hated hot, humid days. He hoped he could find an inside job this summer with air conditioning.

Jake was just the opposite. He loved the heat and talked about moving to Arizona one day. He had a new radio in his old Ford pickup and had the station set to the Oldie Goldies of Rock and Roll. Buddy Holly was his favorite and the "King" as far as he was concerned. He just died young or he'd share the limelight with Elvis. Anyone in the truck with him while Buddy sang "That'll Be The Day" had best remain quiet. But, Jake had a streak of humor like his uncle Bob. He had brown hair like his dad and planned to study wildlife in one field or the other. He thought he might move to the southwest where he might find an appropriate curriculum in his junior and senior years.

His pug nose, short stature and good humor made him a popular boy who contrasted with his tall and handsome friend.

Monday after school David stopped and visited with Gin before going back to work in the attic. He figured he could get in a couple of hours before supper. He had stacked more than he thought was possible before knocking off for supper. He was just taking his gloves off when a piece of wood caught his eye. It was something just behind the next box in the stack. He pulled it out. Yes! It looked like the right box and it was loaded with old letters.

David stopped and showed his find to Gin who immediately began sorting through letters.

"I think you've got it!" She happily held the open box on her lap. I'll find it before too long," she said.

"Find what?"

"The letter from Julia's sister."

"What was her name?"

"I don't remember, but I'll know it when I see it."

"Oh. Are there any letters written by Julia's husband?"

"Oh, sure. Don't worry. I'll set some out for you." So saying, she continued looking in each letter.

David watched for at least an hour before running out of patience and heading home for supper. He had to finish his long paper on "The Causes of the Civil War".

Some scholars were trying to sell the idea that it wasn't slavery which brought about the War. To David that was like saying that WWII was not fought because of Hitler's tyranny. Some scholars were trying to appear more erudite in saying the war was really about having as president a man determined to end slavery, *or* that it was just about money. This in spite of the fact that it was Secretary of State Seward who was most vehemently antislavery and Lincoln who—though opposed to slavery—was willing to do *anything* to preserve the Union. The South had had their men in the White House for many years and, now, the southern fire-brands used Lincoln and the new Republican Party as their excuse for separation. They saw the real threat to slavery was the growth of the Republic into new "free" territories such as Kansas, Nebraska and the far west.

David was vehement regarding his views and backed these with facts. Lincoln had done the same in his First Inaugural Address.

CHAPTER 3

Loss

IN THE LATE AFTERNOON, HE hurried to Gin's house. There was a police car parked outside. He ran up the porch steps and into the house worried about Gin. She was fine, sitting in the living room with a couple of city policemen.

"Hi," David blurted to the three seated in the living room.

"David. I called these policemen because someone broke in last night and found the Lincoln letter! Your mom picked it up from the safe deposit box and left it off here yesterday. We don't know how they knew it was here, but they took nothing else."

"Where was it? I mean where did you put it" His heart sank and he felt sick.

"David, I just set it on the living room table. I never gave thought to burglars." She looked to be on the verge of tears.

David quickly stepped over and put his arms around her.

"Don't worry, Gin. We'll get it back," David said. "You say they didn't take any of the other letters?"

"I was just telling these officers. All the letters were scattered over the floor when I came out this morning." Gin lived only on the downstairs floor and had the second floor closed off. But, her room was on the backside of the house.

"I did look carefully at the letters. I'm pretty sure they took only the Lincoln letter."

One of the officers asked David if he'd talked about the Lincoln Letter with anyone. David looked stricken. He admitted he'd mentioned it in History Class recently.

Had he said anything about the wooden box, asked the officer.

David couldn't say for sure but doubted that he had. But, he had mentioned that it was his great-aunt who was giving it to him. But, he might have told only Mr. Hornsby, his history teacher about that. He just wasn't sure. Gin saw that he was looking grey and sick. She broke in saying she'd appreciate it if they could come back and talk to them in a day or so. Maybe something would come to mind that would help.

The officers agreed and excused themselves. It was obvious that David was more than upset with the loss of the Lincoln letter. Later, he realized he hadn't remembered to tell them he'd told Jake and Bob about the Letter. If it mattered. He'd told a whole class about it! It was probably all over school by now.

In the following two days, nothing came to light. He was so depressed and miserable about the missing Lincoln letter that his teachers noticed. Mr. Hornsby talked to him after the last History Class asking if he'd found the Lincoln letter. He really seemed to feel sorry for David. When he learned about the break-in at Aunt Gin's place he said nothing.

Later that day he received a call at home. It was a reporter from the local paper who'd heard ". . . something about an Abraham Lincoln Letter . . . did he know anything about this?" David declined to talk about it and hung up.

All of which didn't bring back Lincoln's Letter. David considered the problem. Would the letter show up in some auction or in the news? He wondered. What should he look for? And, if it did turn up, how could he prove it came from Gin's home? In other words, how would he prove that *that letter* was *his letter*?

School came to an end and nothing had changed. He wandered out to the porch swing to study on the problem. He'd carried the old helmet with him. Then, for some reason he lifted the helmet and re-examined it.

It was old. Really old. It reminded him of the Middle Ages and knights and the helmets they'd worn in the pictures in his history book. He realized it was inlaid with what looked like gold and silver and made of some metal he couldn't identify. And it had a carved brim and scroll work all over.

He made up his mind. This was going to a specialist for appraisal! Losing the Lincoln Letter was enough. He'd check this out with someone who might have an idea what it was. And, what it might be worth.

CHAPTER 4

A Hint

NEXT MORNING HE HEADED OVER to the school to see if Mr. Hornsby might still be around.

He found the classroom door unlocked and went into the classroom expecting Mr. Hornsby to be there. The room was empty. He wandered up to his desk and glanced at the desk's surface. A paper caught his eye. *"Lincoln's Letter"* was emblazoned across the top of a paper. Not hesitating, he picked it up. That was as far as he got. David stood stock still. Who wrote this? He turned a page to find a name when Mr. Hornsby entered the room.

"Hey! Dave, you know better than that," and he reached out for the paper. David had not seen the name of the writer but had no choice but to hand it to Hornsby. "Now, Dave, you know that everyone has heard about your loss. This paper proves nothing. You put the idea into everyone's head so don't jump to conclusions."

David knew he was right. The paper proved nothing. Except that . . . He needed to know who had written it and what it said.

Somehow he'd figure a way to find out who had written "Lincoln's Letter" on that paper. Maybe his buddy, Jake, would have an idea.

In fact, it was easy. He and Jake just checked with a few of the students in the class and, sure enough, they got the name of the student. It was Cynthia White's paper! She'd not said a word to David about it. He knew, though, that she'd not had a thing to do with the missing letter. One thing he knew for sure, Cynthia was absolutely honest! She was also going to be valedictorian at graduation.

David was unsure she could have written a paper based on what he'd said in class. But, he talked incessantly about Lincoln and that letter. He wasn't sure what she could have written, but it was possible. She had a great imagination and was really smart!

Well, for sure someone had taken it . . . *broken in* and taken it! How had they known where to go? How would they have known to go to Aunt Gin's place? How many people even knew he had an Aunt Gin? And what would you do with such a rare document?

OK, *where would* you go if you had a rare and valuable piece of correspondence? EBay? Well, that was pretty public and probably unlikely, if you'd stolen the item. Would you go to the Internet for information regarding selling it? Very possible if you were computer literate. Well, who wasn't these days?

David talked it over with Jake and came to the conclusion that, if it hadn't been sold, it could be reclaimed one way or another. He wanted that letter in his hands. How to prove it was his?

Cynthia was shocked when they met with her outside the school library and explained the issue. She'd not told David about doing a paper about Lincoln.

"Guys," she said, "you're just way off base. I wouldn't think of stealing something like that! Especially from you, David."

"Cynthia, I believe you. Absolutely. My concern is did you tell anyone else? I mean someone who might be capable of stealing it? That's the thought that bothers me." Cynthia turned white and sat down on a stone seat built into an abutment and was shaking.

"What is it Cynthia?" David sat down beside her.

Then, it came out. Cynthia had an uncle who was a "jailbird" as she termed it. He'd been in prison.

"His name is Max. Max Stark. But . . . I just can't imagine he would do such a thing. We all thought he was on the straight and narrow. He's actually a *step-uncle*. He even has a job, I think."

"Would he have known about the letter?" asked Jake.

She thought for a minute and looked even more pale. "Yes. He was there when I was telling Mom and Dad about what David said in class. You said that President Lincoln had written a letter to a widow named *Julia.* Her husband had done some heroic deed in battle and had been killed."

David's heart sank. Had he said all that?

"Cynthia. Did I really mention her name?"

"Oh, yes! I thought it was such a lovely name. And the mystery of what her husband did in battle to cause President Lincoln to write her just seemed to be a wonderful start to a term paper about the Battle of Antietam . . ."

"Did I say it was a mystery?"

"You said there was a great mystery about the Battle. That you hoped the letter might shed light on it."

"So, you think it might be possible that your uncle could have picked up on what you said . . . . but, how would he have known where to go to find the letter?" David looked doubtful.

"Well, I mentioned your name." Cynthia blushed.

"I still don't see how he'd have known where to go to find that letter. Why, he'd almost have to have followed my mother from where it was stored in the safety deposit box! How would that have been possible? So . . . who knows how it went. Anyhow, he's a possibility. Thanks, Cynthia," David said.

Cynthia was a girl that everyone in school knew about. She was not beautiful but was very pretty, or so thought the boys David knew. She was very unpopular with some students and some teachers. She was unchallenged as valedictorian; her grades were tops in the school. In debates she took on unpopular topics such as "Politically Correct Speech" which she argued had been transmitted by the Soviet Union to the Western World, especially, and ironically, to the U.S. She argued against abortion. She opposed gun control saying that it was a moral responsibility for one to defend their own life and the lives of their families. She laughed at the idea you could "control" guns. How, she would argue, would you disarm the drug dealer, the crook, or the gangs? And, why would you find it even halfway reasonable to disarm the citizenry and not those who lived outside the law.

As the two boys walked away from the library, David's mind turned back to the problem of selling the letter. Where would the thief take the letter for evaluation and sale? What could he say to explain how he came to possess it? Maybe he could find a crooked vendor and pass it on like crooks did counterfeit money.

Jake said "Dave, I don't see any way but to tail Max and see if he goes to a store for rare documents or some such thing. But, he's had it for . . . maybe, three or four days?" David was looking glum but couldn't think of anything else. They couldn't call every rare documents dealer in the city . . . or could they. It was a small city after all. How many could there be? But, what if the crook had gone to Chicago or New York!

When David arrived at home he immediately picked up the phone book. He was supposed to be looking for a job. Jake had been looking, too, without success. Jobs were hard to come by. But, he knew that Mom would be keeping a close eye on him, so he couldn't just hang around the house. And Gin was no better. Getting a job seemed to be the greatest priority at the moment.

There were only three or so rare document dealers. He called the first one on the list, "AA Rare Documents and Antiquities". Whoever answered the phone was obviously in a hurry but asked David what he needed.

"Well, sir, I'm looking for my Lincoln letter. I just wondered if you could tell me if anyone has brought in a Lincoln letter for evaluation or sale?"

"Why do you call here?" said the voice.

"Someone has stolen my Lincoln Letter, and I'm trying to find it. And you guys are listed first in the phone book."

"Young man, I think you should come in for a talk. But be prepared to tell us more about that letter and why it is your property."

"OK. I'll come in first thing tomorrow." David couldn't believe he'd hit pay dirt on the first call! But, maybe that made sense. The thief would probably have gone to the first dealer listed. This might pay off. Could the thief really have been that stupid?

Cynthia seemed to have a low opinion of Max, so maybe he was just dumb.

He made sure he had the address . . . "AA Rare Documents and Antiquities". Say, why not take that helmet along and see what they thought . . .

CHAPTER 5

The Firm

DAVID HAD TO GO ALONE as Jake was going with Bob to check on a possible job. That might turn into a big problem thought David. Jake would be a big help in tracking the letter. He had his old Ford pickup for transportation, too.

He got off the bus and walked into a skyscraper which was really impressive with black slate stone everywhere. He had to ride the elevator to the tenth floor and immediately faced the door labeled "AA Rare Documents and Antiquities." He walked in with his bag under his arm. A lady named Josephine met him and called someone named "Owen" on the intercom.

A tall, elderly man walked to the wooden gate and asked if he could help. David looked up at him guessing the man to be at least six-four in height.

"I called yesterday regarding a lost Lincoln letter. My name is David Thornton."

The towering white haired man looked at him appraisingly and opened the wooden gate motioning David to follow. He was led to the rear to an office where the man sat behind a large desk cluttered with papers.

"So, you lost a Lincoln letter did you," said the tall man. "Tell me about it."

David started at the beginning and told him everything, including his talk with Cynthia.

The man behind the desk frowned. He remained quiet and deep in thought.

Finally, he aroused himself saying "David, I think your letter came in here for evaluation the other day. The fellow had a good story, but we had some doubts and declined to do an evaluation or to make an offer."

David looked downcast wondering how he'd ever get his Lincoln letter back.

"Look here, young man . . . er, David, I wish I could help you. My name is Owen Hagenfenig. Now, that's a mouthful, so you just call me Owen, and I'll call you David, if that's OK . . ."

David felt comfortable with this man, and was greatly impressed that he, or his firm, had declined to make an offer on the Lincoln letter simply because they had doubts about the man who'd brought it in. That smacked of honesty. This man was probably in his sixties, dressed in an immaculate black suit and had rosy cheeks and brown eyes.

"I did call the police and left a message to have them call me. They haven't so far, so I'll call Frank again and report what you've said."

"Aunt Gin and I have already talked to two cops, er. policemen. We talked to them the day after the theft from her house."

"Nonetheless, I'll call them again. Well, if there is nothing else . . ."

Then David thought of the helmet on his lap and pulled it out of the shopping bag. "I was given this helmet by my great-aunt. I just don't know if it's worth anything." He handed the helmet to Owen. Owen set it on the desk staring and apparently speechless. Finally, his stare lifted from the helmet to David. "You were given this by your great aunt? How did she get it," he asked.

David explained how he'd found it sticking out of the insulation in the attic of the old house, and Gin said she had no idea where it came from. She had simply said that he could have it. Neither one knew anything about its value. She'd been living in the house for over fifty years, so it had to have been in the old insulation for over fifty years.

Owen gazed at David in open-mouthed wonder. Finally, he lifted the helmet turning it around so as to view every aspect of the head piece. "David, what you have found is extremely valuable. Much more valuable than the Lincoln letter, I'd think!"

David was shocked. How could that old thing be more valuable than a letter written by Abraham Lincoln? It didn't seem possible.

"How much do you think?"

"David, I can't give you a figure right now. I'll have to have one of my specialists go over this and do a few tests. But, it will be a lot. Now we need to do several things. We have to give you a receipt for the helmet in order to do an evaluation and inspection. Then, we'll need to put an ad in the newspapers requesting anyone who is claiming ownership to appear with evidence supporting their claim. And, we have to alert museums. It will take some time. Now, I have no doubt that you are the legitimate owner. Therefore, I am prepared to give you and your aunt a check as a *tentative* down-payment. Perhaps your aunt will reconsider when she hears what it may be worth?"

"No, sir. My great-aunt will simply refuse. She will tell you that she gave it to me."

David was still in a state of shock but nodded his head emphatically.

"Let's say we meet with your aunt and your parents and discuss this in say four days."

"Sure. Mom will be floored; she thought it was just a piece of junk. My folks are separated, so my dad can't be here. It'll just be my mom and aunt Gin. Whatever it's worth will just go into my savings for college, of course. And, you would be doing me a favor if you called her to explain what you've told me."

"Oh. That's no problem. I'll call today. What do you want to do in college?"

"I want to take courses so I can work with old documents and antiquities."

"Have you got a summer job?" Owen was scribbling on a piece of paper, but stopped and looked up when David replied.

"No, sir. I've been looking, though. A little . . ."

"Well, I've been looking for a young feller to give us a hand this summer. Would you consider working here?"

David was flabbergasted and couldn't say yes fast enough.

"OK. You'll start in ten days on Monday. You can report here at 8 AM, and Josephine will get you started. You'll be on probation for six weeks and will, of course, have to take a drug test. You won't mind if most of your duties entail manual work? You'll be working inside unless you're picking something up or dropping it off. We use a delivery van. You do drive?," he asked.

"Yes, sir!"

"Now, back to your helmet. It will remain *your* helmet until someone else proves ownership or until you decide whether you'll take our offer. And, we'll need your folk's release. You may do better elsewhere. Therefore, if you decide to sell elsewhere you'll owe us the advance we'll furnish plus cost of the evaluation. Do you understand?"

"Yes sir!" David felt like he was in a new and exciting world. To work here in such an establishment left him stunned.

"Fine. Now all of this will be reduced to written format. Our offer will be made when you report to work, I hope. It will depend on responses we get when we alert the museum world. But that goes fast. Not many museums are missing a helmet like your's. And, yes, I'll call your mom."

"One last thing, sir. What did that fellow look like who brought in my Lincoln letter?"

"I was not here when he left the document. I did meet him when we returned it. He did call himself Max but I don't immediately recall what last name he used. He is middle-aged, has grey hair, had his nose broken sometime or another, has a badly scared face and is a heavy five-foot six or seven inches and looks like a jailbird . . . ." laughed Owen.

CHAPTER 6

Police

DAVID WAS FLOATING ON AIR and couldn't wait to tell Mom and Gin the great news . . . an expensive helmet and a job to boot! And working in a company that dealt with old documents and antiquities. Life was good! Owen's call to Mrs. Thornton didn't come until that evening after David had a chance to tell her and Gin about his visit to the antiquities firm.

Gin felt it called for a celebration and invited Jake. Jake suggested to David that Cynthia be invited. David invited Mr. Hornsby. And. of course, David's mom was there. It was a happy celebration. David declined to talk about the helmet. This would just be a small celebration of his graduation. He felt like he'd learned a lesson the hard way. His big mouth had got him into enough trouble. He didn't mention Max, the Lincoln Letter, or the helmet.

David was able to find a private moment and asked Cynthia about her uncle and found out where he lived.

"Oh, David. Be careful! He's got a violent streak in him. What do you plan?"

"The only thing I can think of is to go to the police; Gin already reported the theft. And, Owen reported the attempted sale to the police. Let's find out what they're doing."

"Is that an invitation to go with you?"

"Only if you can drive us there."

"Done."

And, so, the following day David found himself being chauffeured to the city police headquarters by Cynthia in her folk's fancy Olds.

The entrance was guarded by a glassed-in area with an officer on duty behind the glass.

"Could you tell me how to get in touch with an Officer Frank? I think he works in special affairs or something. I don't know his last name. I had a rare document swiped."

"Just a minute." He called someone on the phone and had them take a seat in front of the glass after taking their names.

Within five minutes an officer came towards them from a side entrance.

"I'm Officer Frank Tubbs from Special Affairs. What can I do for you?"

"My name is David Thornton and this is my friend, Cynthia White. I had a letter written by Abraham Lincoln which was stolen about a week ago. I got in touch with Mr. Hagenfenig at AA Rare Documents and Antiquities. He said the letter was brought to his establishment by a guy named Max, an ex-con. His last name is Stark."

"Come with me, please." The officer turned and retreated the way he'd come. He led them through a door and into a wide hallway lined with doors. At the fourth door on the left, he halted, opened the door and motioned them in closing the door behind him. He walked around and sat at an old desk cluttered with papers. It was a small room and seemed odd in such a large building.

"Take a seat, please. Now, how did you happen to go to Owen's firm?"

"It was the first one in the phone book. He says he called you about this."

"Yes. I talked to him yesterday and issued a warrant for Max Stark. He says you know something about the guy."

"He'd a step-uncle. Actually, he is a step-brother of my dad. I have the address of where he was staying if you want it." Cynthia spoke with confidence and held her chin up.

"It seems like quite an odd coincidence that your uncle swiped a letter belonging to your boyfriend."

This caused Cynthia's face to redden, but she didn't hesitate in replying.

"We were classmates in high school. I'm afraid that Max found out about David's letter through my carelessness."

"I see. Well, I'd appreciate getting the address you have. I suspect he may no longer be there, but we'll check."

"I was curious why you didn't return Mr. Hagenfenig's call the first time he tried to alert you?" David spoke in a friendly fashion hoping to avoid confrontation.

"Mr. Thornton, we are not a perfect organization. I apologize to you for the slip-up.

I wish I had called Owen when I got the memo he'd called. Only Max could be dumb enough to go to a reputable dealer like Owen with that letter . . . er, sorry miss."

"No. That's O-K. Max is dumb. Only my dad has any patience with him." Cynthia was shaking her blonde hair while showing a smile.

"What do you think the chances are for retrieving my letter?"

"Mr.—May I call you David? And, I'm Frank." He extended an open hand to David and then to Cynthia. David decided he liked the man.

"I have to tell you that if it is *just* Max, we should have a better than average chance of getting your letter. These ex-cons are pretty sly. I'll do the best I can."

Later, as they were walking back to the car, David shook his head in frustration.

"I know that man was honest. He'll do the best he can, but I'd sure like a 'better than average chance'. That letter is terribly important to me. No one knows how important!"

"I know you're really involved with the Civil War and Mr. Lincoln, but what makes this letter more important than, say, some other Lincoln letter?" She started the car and pulled out into traffic.

So, David revealed his suspicion about the Lincoln letter which had mention of "cigars" as Gin seemed to recall. Then, he told her the story about the Rebel Battle Plans wrapped around *three cigars* before the battle of Antietam. And, before he knew it, he was telling her about his interest in being a scholar researching the issue and McClellan's relationship with Mr. Lincoln, his Commander-In-Chief.

"And, for a Lincoln letter, it is somewhat long. That alone makes it unusual. Well, I suppose you think it is a waste of good time. But I desperately want to do research on the issue. And, I want to study rare documents and antiquities."

Before he knew it, he'd formed a bond with Cynthia and went on to reveal his experience with the helmet.

"It looks like it might make me somewhat solvent. Or, maybe, more than that. I'll know soon."

"David, that's wonderful! Will you be going to college here in town?"

"Yes. That's my plan. At least for the first two years."

"Me, too. What will Jake do?"

"Oh. Jake is doing the same."

The next day David set his mind to locating Max. Cynthia had the address. It was a cheap hotel not too far away. He rode his bike hoping to see the '62 blue Impala Cynthia said he drove. No luck. He walked into the old hotel and went up to the desk.

"Excuse me. I wonder if you could tell me if my uncle, Max Stark, is registered here?"

The clerk looked at him strangely. "Well, the police asked the same question. He checked out two days ago. I have no idea where he went."

"Oh. Well thanks anyway." He wanted to ask more but couldn't think of anything that would make sense, so he turned and walked out.

He decided to ride straight ahead to a district that had many stores and businesses. Twenty minutes later he spotted the old blue Impala. It was parked in front of a large brick business advertising a swimming pool and gym. Bright! He should have at least tried to keep the old vehicle somewhat out of sight . . . if it was his Impala.

David shook his head. What now? Where would he keep it? In the car? How long would he be here? All questions and no answers. If he had Jake, they might be able to do something. He waited. Then, it dawned on him that he should call Officer Frank. He used his cell phone and eventually was connected to the police department. He asked, to be connected to Officer Tubbs. He wasn't in. Then, he reported to the operator that he knew where Max Stark was and that a warrant was out for his arrest. Max was there for just over an hour. No police arrived. David watched helplessly as the stout, scar-faced Max came out, and the Impala moved into traffic and disappeared.

CHAPTER 7

The Room

T HE NEXT MORNING JAKE DROVE to David's house in his old pickup, and they went to the brick building where David had seen the Impala.

No Impala in sight. Jake pulled into a space in front of the building.

"Jake, I've got to go in and have a good story about "my uncle" Max. A story that will give us his address."

"Good luck!"

"So, no brilliant ideas. O-K."

"Well, we could call the cops."

"Jake, I'm kind of sore about them. Where were they when I called yesterday? Right now I'm inclined to trust myself in finding Max and my letter."

"Well, if you figure out a way to get his address, you'll be on the way . . . maybe."

Twenty minutes went by in silence. Jake decided he'd go across the street and get a milkshake. David was lost in thought.

When Jake returned to the truck it was empty.

In only a few minutes David came whistling out of the brick building.

"O-K. So, you got brilliant. How'd you do it?"

"Simple, my man. I just told them my 'dad' had sent me down to pay more on his account. They couldn't get the records out fast enough. Turns out that Max only had a couple more sessions. So,

I paid him up for thirty days. In doing so, I made sure they had his correct address. It wasn't the hotel. He paid a few days at a time. He was dumb enough to put his new address down. I hope."

"Wow! I'm impressed. So what did it cost you?"

"Thirty bucks. And well worth it!"

"What's his address? And, where'd you come by thirty bucks?"

"He's kept to the same neighborhood. Wouldn't you know! And, where is *my* milkshake?"

"Wanted you to keep your nice slim shape, so I sacrificed for you," laughed Jake.

"Figures. Well, here is his new address. Let's mosey over there."

They saw the old blue Impala when they turned the corner of the residential neighborhood. He apparently was renting a room from the landlord as there was a sign reading "Rooms For Rent" planted in the yard.

"Just for kicks, let's see what they want for a room."

"Are you kidding?"

"Nope. It might come in handy." David was already going up the sidewalk,

He rang the doorbell and was answered by a matronly lady who was examining David carefully.

"Yes. Can I help you?"

"Well. My friend, Jake, and I have just graduated from high school and are looking for our first room. We wondered what you charge?"

"Well, I've never rented to anyone yer age. I can't put up with parties and sech. I do have a room with two beds. One is a cot. The other is a single mattress bed. Bathroom's down the hall. Have to share with the other renter. I need $175.00 a month and a deposit."

"Great! Could I look at it?"

Jake looked with wonder as David disappeared into the house with the woman. After a fifteen minute wait, the door opened and David was laughing at something the woman was saying.

"How do you do it?"

"Do what?"

"Charm your way through life! Why do they believe you!"

"My honest charm goes a long way. I looked at the room she has for rent. Only $175.00 a month. That's $87.50 for you and you get the cot. Best of all, it's the room next to Max."

"How on earth did you get that out of her?"

"Why, with perfect honesty. I just asked who our neighbor was. She described him as a wonderful gentleman who had been mauled by a bear years ago and was terribly scared. But, he will be a quiet neighbor. He is seldom even in his room," she says.

"You sound as if you rented the room."

"I did."

"You did what?"

"I rented the room."

Jake pulled the truck over to the curb. "Dave, how are we going to pay her $175.00?"

"You forget about the deposit."

"Where's all this money coming from?"

"Oh. I guess I didn't tell you. I sold the helmet."

"What helmet?"

"The one I found."

"You found it. Where did you find a helmet that's worth $175.00?"

"Actually, it is worth more than two-hundred thousand dollars. I was paid $3,500.00 as a down payment while it's being appraised. So, $175.00 for a chance to check Max's room for my Lincoln letter is a bargain. I gave her a check in that amount plus $75.00 deposit."

Jake sat in stunned silence.

"I guess I should have told you. I found an exquisite old helmet—actually, one from the Middle Ages—while I was searching for Gin's letters up in her attic. It was just sticking out of the insulation between rafters. She had no idea where it came from and gave it to me. I took it to *AA Rare Documents and Antiquities*. Turns out it is worth more than $225 thousand dollars. We don't have a final offer, yet. My mom and aunt Gin went with me to the firm, and we accepted a check for $3,500.00 in advance. So, my bank account is looking pretty good at the moment."

Jake remained silent. Finally, he shook his head. "Well, you can afford to put some gas in this rig and buy *me* a milkshake!"

"I'll do more than that. How would you like to work for me? Say, at ten dollars an hour?"

"Plus milkshake breaks?"

"Yes. I think that would work." So, David became an employer.

CHAPTER 8

The Locker

NOW WHAT? MAX HAD A strange job that allowed him to go out at ten o'clock in the morning and come back to his room in two hours. Today, he'd been gone only a bit over one hour and that had been spent in a bar. David began to believe that Max did not have a job. The Letter might be his mother lode just waiting to get cashed in.

Where was the letter? David had had no trouble entering Max's room. The old door had an old fashioned key like the one on their room. With only a few jiggles of his own key he had the door open. He'd searched the room thoroughly while Jake sat on watch in his truck. If Max returned, he'd call David on his cell phone.

The real problem was dealing with David's mom. What was he doing? She was worried and not about to let him just come and go at all hours. She made it clear the she'd rest a lot better when he started to work for Mr. Hagenfenig.

It seemed like today might be the day to keep a close eye on Max. He'd be uneasy about that letter. As an old con he'd be suspicious of everything and everyone. He'd be wondering who had paid his gym bill for thirty days. He was sly enough to surely know it had something to do with his only item of value . . . the letter. So, would he keep it in his room? It didn't seem likely. At least he'd had no luck in his search.

David explained his reasoning to Jake. "Max won't feel safe keeping the letter in his room. He's an old con. He'll get it to a safe place . . . as safe as he can find. I think it's time to follow him."

They had just driven up to the house as the blue Impala was moving away from the curb. But, they were headed the wrong direction. Jake was able to get turned around using a driveway but the Impala was out of sight. They drove straight on to the small business section just as David had done on his bike. It took them past the swimming pool and gym and out toward an industrial area. They crossed railroad tracks but still no blue Impala. After an hour of driving around without seeing the Impala, they returned to the house.

There was the Impala. Darn! David was frustrated. Where had he gone? Had he gone to a bank and got a safe deposit box? If so, they were out of luck. Jake suggested a locker at a bus depot which was quickly dismissed as there was no bus depot. Where else would there be a locker?

"Maybe a railroad station," suggested Jake.

"We passed the railroad station," David exclaimed.

They walked into the old railroad station. There were lockers.

That night Jake stayed over at David's place sleeping on the couch in David's "office." They were eating breakfast the next day when David said "That's the only way!"

"What is," Jake asked through a mouthful of Wheaties.

"Tell you later, Pal."

"Boys, I know you've been trying to get that Lincoln letter back, but you two be careful!" Mrs. Thornton was letting them know she wasn't completely dumb.

After she drove off for work, David explained. "Look here, Jake. We have to find where he's left that letter. Now, I can get into his room. Could he be carrying a locker key in his pocket? If he has, how can we get it and stay out of jail? Well . . . what can you think of that will allow us to find out if he has a locker? Jake, we're going to need a lot of luck. If he's used a safety deposit box or something, we're out of luck. But, I think you may have hit on it. The locker keys at the train depot are easy to identify."

"Great! But what now?"

"Jake, there has to be some way. Think!"

CHAPTER 9

The Key

"LET'S GET BACK TO THE room, Jake". David was nervous about not knowing what Max was up to; he might have contacted a buyer and retrieved the Letter by now. What did he do all day? He obviously didn't have a job. What was he doing for money? Was someone supplying him with money? Maybe his step-brother?

The Impala was still parked where it had been before. David heaved a sigh of relief.

"You ought to smell that car!" Jake said. "It smells like vomit."

Now what? They waited in the room until it began to get dark. It was a worry. They couldn't wait all night. David had brought in an old TV from home but they only got local stations. It turned into a long day.

Finally, as they were about to give up, Max left his room and went out to his car. They followed just in time to see the Impala move out into the street. Jake was unable to catch up, had lost sight of the blue car. They couldn't see the car but went by the swimming pool and gym and drove to the bar where he'd gone before. There was the Impala.

David was disgusted. He was running out of time. He had to start work Monday morning and this was Friday. "OK, Jake. Let's go back to the room."

"Why," asked Jake.

"Well, I think we'll have to do this the old fashioned way," David groaned. "We're just running out of time."

"Let's discuss this a bit, Dave." Jake was clearly uncomfortable.

"Just take me back to the room. I'll figure out a way of getting the key there. He has to sleep sometime. You'll have the tough job. If you can come back here and keep an eye on him, I'll get into his room. If he leaves here and gets the letter at the train depot, you're going to have to follow him to see where he takes it."

"This sounds pretty dangerous, Dave. I mean your waiting in his room. What if he finds you there?"

"I know. But we have to have that key. I just can't think of another way to get it. If he drinks as much as it appears he does, then he may just pass out when he comes back."

Jake snorted. "Yeah! And what if he just lies down without taking off his britches? Then what?"

Dave didn't know. But he couldn't think of anything else. "Let's go, Jake."

Jake was just about to say 'no' when he heaved a sigh and started the truck. He dropped Dave at the house and turned back towards the bar.

David walked into the house and listened for the matron. No sounds at all. He jiggled the skeleton key in Max's door but couldn't get it open. Max couldn't possibly have changed his lock. Then, it clicked and he was in! He took a chance, turned on the bedside lamp and checked the drawers. They looked the same with not much in the way of contents. No key.

He dropped to his knees and lay down squirming under the bed. He went to the back wall and pulled his feet up as far as possible. He could just see Max tripping on his legs when he came in . . . that'd be great!

Except for feeling like he was in a dust bin and occasionally feeling cramped, it wasn't too bad. Still he thought the man would never come. Maybe he wouldn't! What if he'd found a way to get arrested or something. I just can't see staying here all night, he thought. And, he could just see his mom; by midnight she'd be calling the cops.

When he was sure it must be coming on to dawn, he heard the key going into the lock. Max sounded like he was stumbling and sagged onto the bed where he kicked off his shoes and tugged down his pants leaving them in a heap on top of the shoes. Only a bit of light made its way through the blinds on the window, but it showed the pile of discarded clothes.

David wrinkled his nose smelling something . . . stale booze. Then, Max was snoring. He wriggled over to the clothing on the floor and felt something sticky on the pants. Ugh! Was this the vomit Jake had talked about? He searched each pocket but found only the car keys . . . only two identical keys. No locker key. Where had he put it? What if he left it in the car or had hid it somewhere. Wouldn't that be great!

Then he pulled the wallet from the gooey pants. Was there a coin pocket? He felt something in the thin wallet. Yes! He pulled a short key from the coin pocket.

He returned the wallet to the pocket and squirmed out from under the bed trying to avoid the sticky pants. He slipped out of the room, returning to his room where Jake sat doubled over in laughter. "Dave! How'd it go?"

"Got it, David said holding the key up, but he must have heaved all over his pants!"

Jake resumed laughing. "Oh, I love it," he groaned.

"What's so funny?"

Jake said, "Oh, he did take his pants off didn't he," and relapsed into hysterics.

David was looking at Jake in irritation. What was this? "'OK, Jake what's so funny?"

"I threw a milkshake at him when he staggered out of the bar," Jake snorted.

"You did what?"

"I got a strawberry milkshake and when he came out of the bar, I was standing by the doorway. As soon as he got past me I threw the milkshake at him. Got him good!"

"What did he do," asked David.

"He just stopped in his tracks, and I ran like hell!" Jake was laughing again.

"Jake, you're a genius! The first thing he did was leave those trousers on the floor. They were right in front of my nose!"

Soon, the pickup was moving down the street, and both knew where they were going. It was just eleven o'clock. David was amazed. He'd have sworn it was two AM or later.

They pulled into the parking lot and almost ran into the train depot. It took only minutes before they'd located locker number 114 and had the key into the lock. It was empty.

CHAPTER 10

Duplicate

DAVID WAS UP EARLY. IT was going to be a busy week. He was puzzled. Why had that locker been empty? Try as he would he just couldn't find a time when Max could have picked it up. And still have the key! Could he have taken it somewhere else? But he'd have had to leave the key in the locker. So why the locker? No. He must have used the locker for something. If the "something" had been picked up, there had to be a duplicate key.

Jake showed up asking if David had any ideas. No, he hadn't but wanted to go back to the depot.

David walked into the depot and went to the counter where he stood in a short line. "Yes," asked the clerk.

"I want to know what happens if I need a second key for a locker."

"What do you mean? Why would you need a second key?"

"Well, if I lose my key, how would I get my stuff?"

"Oh. You'd just go to the lost luggage office over there," and he waved at an office across the lobby.

He crossed the lobby and entered the Luggage Office. The girl behind the counter was tying a tag to a suitcase. She asked what she could do. He posed the same question he'd asked the counter man. "Oh. I have a key which will open all the lockers."

"But what if it's in the middle of the night?" She looked at him curiously and asked if he'd lost his key.

"No. Just wondered what I'd have to do if I did lose it," David said, trying not to look like a complete idiot. "I mean, what if someone were watching and had a duplicate key?"

"Well, he couldn't have keys to all the lockers, so . . ." She was looking at him closely as if he were a complete squirrel.

"OK. But could he get a copy made of my locker key?" David wasn't giving up.

"Yes. It's supposed to be against the law for a key shop to make copies of locker keys, but I guess someone would do it." And, she turned away in dismissal.

As he stepped into Jake's old Ford he explained what he'd found out in the depot.

"Why would it matter?"

"It would matter if Max had a partner," David suggested.

Jake remained silent as they drove back to David's place. Then, before getting out, he turned to David asking, "Who do you think that might be?"

"It'd have to be someone he trusted, and someone who might be able to sell the letter . . . a person who knows something about it. And someone with the extra key to the locker."

Jake looked doubtful. "Let's say you're right. How would an ex-con find such a person? Not at the local library, for sure. I mean, what do we really know about Max?"

David had a quick response. "He's from a good family, or at least, is a part of a good family. We know that. I think we need to talk to Cynthia."

"I think you've seen quite a bit of her lately," grinned Jake. "Call her on the cell," he said starting the truck. "By the way, what would she know?"

"Well, she is his niece . . . sort of. Anyway, he heard of the letter through her. Maybe he found out about some expert through her. What have we got to lose by asking . . . ," David vaguely thought he'd missed something.

Jake interrupted by saying, "Make the call."

They were soon pulling up before Cynthia's house. It was a mansion! Big. Big as a public library David thought. She was waiting outside. She led them inside the house where Mrs. White asked if they'd like a snack. They declined and followed Cynthia into a living room large enough to fit David's entire house.

CHAPTER 11

Max's Partner

S HE WAS DYING TO KNOW the latest, and sat beside David on the huge circular couch. He filled her in on the whole episode at the rental house and the train depot. He was still upset about the empty locker. Max had a key yet the locker was locked and required a key to unlock it. So, why was the locker still locked? There had to be another key. The other person would have had to take the contents out and have inserted coins in order to relock it and take the key. Why would anyone relock an empty locker? Was it Max? If so, why?

Cynthia looked thoughtful and said "Perhaps someone was stealing it from Max. How did they get the extra key? Or, was there an extra key?"

David looked startled and asked Jake if he'd seen any familiar figure enter the bar last night.

"Well, no. But it was pretty dark. I was only looking for Max to come out. But I was gone for ten or fifteen minutes to get milkshakes."

David turned to Cynthia saying "I think you have something there. Someone stealing from Max . . . it makes as much sense as anything. Still, why relock an empty locker?"

Cynthia suddenly exclaimed, "I'll bet Max doesn't even know . . ."

"Know what? That he's been ripped off? He sure knows that his key is missing," David said.

"But why wouldn't Max be able to get the guy?," asked Jake.

"In jail, he couldn't," exclaimed Cynthia, "and he is back in jail! Dad got a call from him this morning. Now, you can bet he'd not squeal on someone. He'd plan on revenge, but he'd never squeal, or only as a last resort!"

"Back in jail . . ." David was stunned. It sure hadn't taken much time.

"Did your dad say what the charges are?"

"Yes. He said Max was picked up for *armed robbery*," Cynthia replied.

"Now, to the million dollar question," Jake said, "who is his partner? And how did they get to know each other? I mean, that partner is someone Max needed . . . an expert in the field."

"Maybe not an *expert* in the field but, at least, someone who could do what he couldn't."

A sort of fence," suggested David.

"OK, does that bring anyone to mind," asked Jake.

"Yes! Yes, it does," said Cynthia.

"Who," the boys spoke in unison.

"How about Mr. Hornsby?"

The boys looked stunned. "Our history teacher?" David was dubious.

"All right. Who can you think of," Cynthia asked.

David had no answer.

"David, you saw a paper on his desk the day after school was over. I had my term paper at home. That had to be something else."

CHAPTER 12

Evaluation

I<small>T WAS GOOD TO HAVE</small> graduation behind him, David thought. Mom and Gin had talked "college" incessantly. "And, you know college will be very difficult if you get married," Gin warned with a mischievous smile.

Monday morning finally arrived and David reported for work. Josephine had him fill out some papers and turned him over to Mr. Willkie. Mr. Willkie assigned him the task of taking waste cans down to the garbage disposal units in the basement.

After garbage, came the moving of boxes to the storage room. He wondered if the boxes were filled with rare documents or artifacts like his helmet. He decided that wasn't very likely.

Before he knew it lunch time came, and he found about twelve people, men and women, in the lunch room. Included was Owen who came in and sat beside David. "How's it going," he asked.

"Fine." He was at a loss for words. Owen was obviously the boss. He wore a suit and tie while everyone else wore casual clothes from Levi's on.

"If you get a chance, drop in and see Will. He's evaluating your helmet. You'll find it interesting." With that, Owen went out of the lunch room. No one seemed to pay attention.

David didn't know who *Will* was but vowed to find out.

Late in the afternoon he had the occasion as he was directed by Mr. Willkie to Wilbur's office.

He approached a small office with Mr. Wilbur Steel printed in black letters on the door. He went in and saw that the office was just a cluttered room with a desk pushed into the corner. Off to the right side was a large piece of plastic running from floor to ceiling from wall to a post and back to another wall. It was all attached to walls, ceiling and floor with duct tape. From the corner away from the plastic came a tall man carrying his helmet. "Come in and grab a chair," he said, moving some books off a straight backed chair. "Understand this is your helmet."

"Yes, sir. And, you're Mr. Steel?"

"Yip. That I am, but call me Will, please."

"What have you found out about the helmet?"

"Well, I've found out it is very old—1400's A.D—very scarce, and very valuable."

"What makes it so valuable?"

"Ah! That's a good question. Let's start with what it's made of . . . a lot gold and silver. Just in weight alone it's valuable. Next, it old and rare. Not for battle. It's for ceremony."

"Why is it so rare?"

"It's rare because not many like this were ever made, if any! It was made for a member of the royalty somewhere in Europe. Now, combine scarcity with valuable metals, exquisite design and artistry with a period or figure in history, and you will have a valuable object. For example, was it made for the King of the Franks?"

"Yeah. I understand so far. How about a letter written by Abraham Lincoln?"

"Simple. It's very rare, has historical value—sometimes—and, often, is beautiful . . . that is, it's written by one of the most gifted writers in history."

"Hey, thanks. I'd better get back to work."

"Anytime," said Wilbur.

CHAPTER 13

Mr. Hornsby

FRIDAY EVENING JAKE DROVE UP in the old Ford and asked what David wanted to do. "Want to keep an eye on Hornsby?" asked David.

"Why?" asked his skeptical friend.

"Because, Cynthia makes good sense," David stoutly maintained.

"Oh, I agree. But what's he going to do?"

"Think about it. Who got in touch with whom *first?* Max or Hornsby?"

Jake stared at David.

"Did Hornsby contact Max to steal the letter in the first place, or did Max hear about Hornsby and contact *him* after the theft? In any case, if Hornsby has the letter, he's had plenty of time to sell it." David was clearly in the dumps.

At this point, Cynthia drove up in her folks Olds. As she walked up the walk to take a seat on the swing, Jake grinned and said, "Just talking about you, Cynthia."

"Talking about me? Was it good or bad?"

"Oh, it was mostly skeptical," laughed David.

"Still don't think Mr. Hornsby's involved," she asked, smiling.

David was instantly alert. Something about her smile was self-satisfied. "What do you know that we don't," he asked.

"I've given the problem a lot of thought—not finding a job that I want—and I've come to some conclusions. Max had to get someone who could market the letter. He tried once and met with a flat refusal. He's not dumb enough to try that again. He's dumb, but there are limits. If he did try it again, the word would get around, and quickly, too. In fact, it has. So, who could he get who might know something about it? Who might he have heard about? Mr. Hornsby."

"How would he have known about Hornsby?" David already knew the answer.

"From me." Cynthia said empathically.

"Why would you have discussed Mr. Hornsby with Max," asked Jake.

"It happened this way. I got a super grade on my paper and was talking to my folks about it. Guess who was there? Max!"

David scratched his head. "OK. But what would lead Max to think Hornsby wouldn't call the cops right off? No, I have a better theory. Mr. Hornsby somehow heard about Max and put him up to stealing the letter. Or, he might have contacted Max after he heard that Max was a suspect. However it happened, I can't see Max approaching a seemingly honest teacher who would most certainly have blown the whistle."

"So, where do we go from here," asked Jake.

"Well, I think what happened might have gone like this. Hornsby put Max up to stealing the letter with a specific buyer in mind. Max tried to do an end run and contacted my firm where he quickly found he was out of his depth. So, he had to go back to Hornsby. Hornsby quickly got his hands on the letter and called the cops on Max. Max could only make things worse by saying he'd swiped the letter." David looked to see the reaction to his analysis.

Both friends agreed that this made sense. True, Max would not have approached the teacher first. It had to be the teacher who contacted Max. And Hornsby knew that Gin was giving the letter to David as a graduation gift.

"Did you ever mention Max to Mr. Hornsby?" asked Jake.

"No, but my dad did," said a startled Cynthia.

"For heaven's sake, why would your dad mention Max," asked David.

"well, we had Mr. Hornsby to supper at the start of the school year. Mom and dad always have a new teacher to dinner at the start of each school year. Mr. Hornsby met Max at our place. Mr. Hornsby was talking to dad after Max left and said he looked familiar and did he graduate from the State University. Dad laughed and said the only graduating Max had done was from the State Penitentiary."

"But, where does this get us," asked Jake.

"Hornsby would have figured on a buyer who would not go public with it," said David.

"Yes, he couldn't sell it on Ebay or public auction. He'd have identified a potential buyer who wouldn't ask where it came from. Mr. Hornsby would know he couldn't be easily touched if the buyer didn't go public with it," Cynthia surmised.

"Why would anyone put out a large sum of money for something he couldn't exhibit," asked Jake.

"Well, take my case," said David, "I just want to hang it on the wall."

"Why would you do that," asked Jake.

"Because, it's part of our family history. Sure, eventually, I'd want it in a museum. And, if there is any historical significance, I'd want that known and published."

"You have heard of those crazy collectors who buy famous paintings that have been stolen? Then, they keep them hidden away in their private collections? There are such people," said Cynthia. "But, let's go back to Mr. Hornsby. In his case, he's just not in a financial position to even have a private collection unless it's going to be a collection of one item! No. Mr. Hornsby would be after the money. As a historian he must have a hard time sleeping nights. But after Max took it in for evaluation, Hornsby would want to get rid of it in any case and fast before it got traced to him."

"How would he find a crooked collector," asked Jake.

"It's surprisingly easy to find a crooked collector. Just look on internet," said Cynthia.

"I checked and found a short list of convicted collectors and their biographies. So, how are you going to contact people on that list? You'd hesitate to do it by phone as there might be a police tap on that phone. Would you drive or fly to contact them? Kind of expensive and could take a lot of time. If it were me, I'd simply write and ask them if they had interest in purchasing a Lincoln letter. I'd put my cell number in the letter and see if they called. And, I'd write only to one collector at a time starting with the nearest."

"Boy! You've got this figured out," said David. "Have you come up with a likely candidate?"

"I've made a very short list of people who you could reach without a coast-to-coast flight. Remember, as rare documents go, this is probably a relatively expensive item."

"Really! How much do you think, boss?" said Jake, looking at David. Cynthia missed nothing of this.

"A personal letter signed by Mr. Lincoln would probably sell for less than $25,000, but that's only a guess," David said. "If it has something unique, or of special historic value, it could go for much more. I think this letter has real historic value. Cynthia, who's on your list of potential buyers?"

"I've put together a list of only three names. One is right here in town! The other is in Chicago. And, there is another who lives about three hundred miles away. David, you work for a rare documents dealer. Would they have an idea who on my list might be most likely to buy the letter?"

"I'd be willing to ask Owen. He'd tell me straight off if he would be willing to do that." He was amazed they'd come to some concrete things to pursue. He only hoped he wasn't convicting an innocent man . . . namely, Mr. Hornsby. Then, a depressing thought crossed his mind. What if Hornsby had sold the letter to some crooked collector? How would he ever be able to get it back?

Then, he said, "Well, one step at a time. I'll see what Owen has to say."

CHAPTER 14

Owen

MONDAY MORNING ARRIVED, AND HE was back at work. His first job was to drive the panel truck with Wilbur to pick up a long list of chemicals. The evaluation of the helmet was still not completed, and David wondered if something was wrong.

As if Wilbur had read his mind, he said "Well, I'm back on your helmet. Sorry I haven't been able to get it finished. Owen had to pull me off for a few days on a rush job."

"What takes so long?"

"We're talking about a lot of money . . . not to mention the reputation of the firm. It's got to be dead-on correct. I can't leave anything on the table. You see, it's my reputation, too. If I make a mistake, it may well be the end of my career."

"What kind of mistakes?"

"There are several possibilities. First, is it a genuine object? Or, is it a fake? If not a fake, was it stolen? From whom? Then, I have to ascertain the value based on several factors before it goes to the committee."

"What's the committee?"

"Owen assembles the entire staff, and they review all the work I've done. I'm present to answer any questions. In the end they say 'aye or nay' to my conclusions and assigned degree of rarity, historical significance and worth. Then, they determine what the firm should offer the owner, if it's for sale. If it's not for sale, the owner is given our estimate of value and is billed for the work we've done. That's pretty much short hand, but it gives you an idea."

"Wow! That's quite a process!" David was impressed.

"Yeah. But don't worry. Your's is genuine. Now, that Lincoln Letter. Wish I could have seen that. Joe got that one and called it off for some reason. I heard it was returned to the customer before it should have been. Have you met Joe?"

"I know who he is but haven't talked to him."

"Well go by and see him. He's sometimes gruff, but he don't bite. Be warned, though. He can't tell you anything about the letter. It's company policy."

Later that afternoon David had occasion to see Joe sitting alone during the coffee break. He took a chance and sat down across from him. Joe looked up, smiled and stuck out his hand which David gratefully shook. "I'm the new errand boy."

"You don't look much like a boy. You must be six foot. What's happening?"

"Will said I might talk to you briefly about the Lincoln letter you turned back."

"Yes?" Joe sounded remote and not much enthused.

"I was wondering what it was that made you stop work on it?"

"David, I'm not at liberty to talk about that. You might touch base with Owen." And, he stood, saying he had to get back to work.

He didn't have to touch base with Owen as Owen asked to see him the next morning.

David was a bit apprehensive because he'd suggested that Will thought he could talk a bit about the Lincoln letter.

"Joe says you asked about the Lincoln letter."

"Yes, sir."

"Well, it may just be a formality, but he is not allowed to discuss a project with anyone unless they are the certified owner. I know that it was a stolen manuscript, but your ownership is not, yet, certified. So, our policy is that we don't discuss a project until ownership is verified and certified."

Looking shame faced, David admitted that he'd told Joe that Will had said he could talk about the letter. "Will did not say any such thing. In fact, he warned me that Joe couldn't talk about it. I just got carried away knowing that the letter is mine."

"Oh, I know that. And I have no doubt that the manuscript is yours. I just want you to know why Joe couldn't talk about it."

"Yes, sir. I wonder if you could assist me in tracking the letter down."

"In what way?"

"Well, sir, I have a list of three names we think might have bought the letter illegally. I thought you might have an idea who is most likely?" He passed Cynthia's list of three names to Owen.

Owen studied the list briefly and said, "David, if I were a betting man, I'd say the man who lives here in town would be the most likely. Doesn't Max still have it?"

"No sir. At least, we're pretty sure he doesn't have it; he's now in jail for armed robbery. We think he had a partner in the theft of the letter."

"You need to talk to Detective Frank Tubbs at the main police department. And, who is this *we* you keep referring to?"

"Oh. I'm sorry. My friends, Jake and Cynthia. They graduated with me. Cynthia is the one who found the names on that list."

"That's pretty impressive work. A smart girl. Well, let's back to work."

"Yes, sir, Mr. Owen!" said David, standing.

"David. No 'Mr.' before Owen, please."

"OK, Mr. Hagenfenig."

"Say! I'm impressed. You'll do well. When you graduate from college I think you'd better come see me!"

"Yes, sir!" David grinned as Owen shook his head smiling.

CHAPTER 15

Police

THE MYSTERY OF THE LINCOLN Letter might extend beyond the letter itself. It might extend to the container which Julia may have put it in. Why would Joe have questioned ownership of the letter and gone to Owen? Joe had never met Max. Josephine had accepted the letter for evaluation.

David discussed the whole matter with Cynthia and Jake. They were as stumped as he. Cynthia suggested that they get with Gin to see if she might be able to shed light on the issue. They all agreed it was a good idea, and Cynthia drove them to Gin's house in the Olds.

Gin was pleased when David showed up with his two friends. They sat in the living room where David explained all that had happened and why they were sure Max had a partner. Finally, he brought up Joe who—for some unknown reason—had not worked with the letter but had gone to Owen who refused to deal further with the customer.

"Why didn't they call the police," asked Gin.

"If they'd had time and Owen had been there when the letter came in, I think they would have, David said. But Mr. Hagenfenig did call the police when he returned from a trip. Gin, we were wondering if Julia, or another descendant, put the letter in another container? Perhaps, with a note? I know that sounds weird, but what was it that made Joe take the letter directly to Owen? And why did Owen immediately contact Max and refuse evaluation of the letter? And, then, call the police?"

"Why don't you ask Owen," asked Gin.

"Well, I did. He says once they can see the letter again and establish ownership they can reveal why they refused service to Max."

"Well, it sounds bureaucratic to me." She remained silent for a moment and added, "I seem to recall something . . . I can't quite remember. It was so long ago. Let me think about it. I'll call you on your cell, David, if I can jar my memory. I'm so sorry I was so careless in leaving the Letter out like that! Say, I have set several of the old letters aside to give you. I think you'll like them!"

"Hey, Gin. I'm the one who opened his big mouth and spread it around school. It's not your fault that someone broke in and took the Lincoln letter. I'm really anxious to look at those letters you've picked out for me. I don't think I deserve them."

"Well, it was my crooked step-uncle who heard me blab about the letter. And it was he who broke in and took it," Cynthia said.

Jake had been silent but said "I've had a few ideas about the thing. Now, if we think that Mr. Hornsby was involved why do we think that Max took it? I mean, maybe, Hornsby decided to steal it when David first talked about in class? And before Cynthia wrote her paper or mentioned it at home in Max's presence."

"It's a thought, but how would Max have got his hands on it? Max was the one who took it in for evaluation," said Cynthia.

"Yes," Gin said, "maybe they were in cahoots from the start? Maybe they had somehow got together and plotted the whole thing? Crooks can do astounding things. And, is Mr. Hornsby any better than Max? A crook is a crook. I do find it odd that Max was so quickly arrested for another crime just when the letter went missing from that locker.

He sure didn't get much out of the whole business. He was just in over his head. I bet Hornsby called the police on Max after he had the letter!"

"Thanks, Gin, you make a lot of sense," David said, standing, and leading his friends to the door. "Give me a call on the cell if anything comes to mind. I think we're hitting close to the truth. I think we ought to check with the police."

Jake was opening the back door of the Olds and said, "Dave, why do you want to go to the police?"

"Jake, a crime has been committed and reported. I was here when the two police officers sat in that living room with Gin and me. Cynthia and I have been to the police already. Nothing has come of it. Now, if we go to the police saying we have proof that Max swiped the letter and, in the process, mention a possible partner . . . maybe we can get them to talk to Max. I mean Max would really be steamed if he thought his partner had turned him in on the armed robbery!"

"Yes. It makes sense. Maybe we can get the police to verify that he had a partner. I mean, who squealed on Max and turned him in? Let's go downtown and see Mr. Tubbs," said Cynthia, turning out into the street.

When they entered the Department they encountered the same police officer seated behind the glass. He politely asked their business.

David spoke saying, "We have information about a crime committed by Max Stark and need to speak to Officer Tubbs."

The Officer turned in his seat and yelled, "Frank. You have some young folks who want to talk to you about Max Stark."

In swift order, Frank appeared and took them behind the glass to his office. "What crime are you talking about," he asked.

"Max swiped my Lincoln letter as we told you before. Then, someone turned him in on the armed robbery crime. Where is my letter? You didn't find it on him or in his room. So, who has it? And, who would profit by turning Max in? We think his partner has the Lincoln letter, and we think that person tipped off you folks about the armed robbery to get Max out of the way," David suggested.

Frank looked surprised and reached for a phone. He dialed a number and said, "Sam, I think you ought to come in here for a minute. Thanks." He hung up the phone and explained that Sam Long was a fellow Detective.

Sam entered the office and sat on the corner of the desk. Frank explained that he'd arrested Max on a tip from an unknown caller. Now these young people were saying Max had tried to market a rare letter with "AA Rare Documents and Antiquities" but was denied. Who had the rare letter? And who had turned Max in?

"Sam, looks like you have some leverage on your mark. If we can get the name of the tipster, we may know who has that letter."

"I'll check it out and give you a call."

Frank looked at David and said "I suppose you're trying to locate your aunt's letter. That's commendable, but go very careful. The fellow who tipped us off about Max could be a very dangerous person. Especially, if he has that letter."

David shifted uncomfortably saying "The thing is, could you let us know who tipped you off about Max . . . I mean, if Max tells you . . ."

"The short, and final, answer is no." Frank got up and showed them out.

CHAPTER 16

Hornsby

LEAVING THE POLICE DEPARTMENT THEY stopped for burgers. Waiting for their orders David said, "don't know what good that did!"

"Not sure, either. But, maybe, it's time Max's name is tied in with a possible partner," said Cynthia.

"Yes. And Max might give up the name of his partner," said Jake.

"What good will that do us," asked David.

"Maybe it will!" She nodded at David, "If you could find out if the police tell Owen who Max's partner is, we could verify that it's Hornsby . . . or not. And, we might be able to check this local guy on our list to see if he has any contact with Hornsby."

"Maybe," said David, "but my concern is that the police want crooks but seldom seem to find the stolen goods."

"Those cops we talked to seem pretty sharp. Maybe something good will come of it," said Jake.

"No problem there, The real concern I have is that you be extremely careful. This could get dangerous real fast! What I have in mind is for you to keep an eye on Hornsby.

He's single, so there should be no problem with a sharp eyed wife spotting you. In regard to a possible buyer of the manuscript, we know, really, nothing for sure. But, it seems likely that Hornsby might have to go to a collector, rather than the collector coming to him. Not sure about that. Anyway, here is Cynthia's list of possible buyers. Only one is local."

"OK, so I stake out Hornsby's place."

"Yes, and keep in touch. I'll worry myself to death as it is! Do you suppose he'd recognize you or your truck?"

"It's possible. He met me at that party at your place."

"Let's hope he doesn't spot you."

Cynthia was looking curiously at David but said nothing.

CHAPTER 17

Surveillance and Revelation

MONDAY CAME AND WENT WITH nothing unusual as David went about his duties. He was worried all afternoon wondering about Jake and what trouble he might be in. It didn't help when Jake finally called just before supper.

"What took you so long! I've been home for two hours," David fairly yelled. A look from his mother drove him out to the front porch.

"Take it easy. It was really a boring day. I kept an eye on his house all day. At about two this afternoon he went to a mall. He bought a handgun in a large sporting goods store, so we know he can pass a background check."

"Jake, I'm really worried, now. You're riding herd on an armed man."

"I doubt I'll ever get closer than a block to the man. Not to worry, Dave."

"Jake, I'll worry! What made him buy a handgun, I wonder?"

"I've been thinking. Do you suppose he wants to be armed when he meets with the collector?"

"I suspect he's already seen the collector. What could be the hang-up? If he sold the letter, why buy a handgun? Unless, they couldn't come to terms . . . Hey, Mom's calling me to eat. You BE CAREFUL!"

An hour after dinner the cell rang. It was Cynthia. She started out complaining about having ". . . nothing to do—I can't find a job I want—and drove out to the address of the local collector on my list".

"You did what! Cynthia you're making me nervous. That could be really dangerous!"

"Oh, it was nothing. I was just curious what kind of house he has. It's very ordinary."

"Cynthia, please don't do that again." David heard the phone go dead. Darn, he thought, darn!

When he arrived home the next day his phone rang. Jake said his day had been boring. Hornsby had only gone to a grocery store.

Cynthia called shortly after saying her day had been boring. This made David suspicious. "What were you doing today?"

"Oh, nothing. I did keep an eye on the collector's house."

"Cynthia, this can't go on. It's dangerous," and he told her about Hornsby buying a gun.

"How did you find out about that," asked Cynthia. So, he told her about hiring Jake. He knew she was aware of the fact but also was aware that he hadn't told her outright.

"Oh! That's right! You're coming into great wealth. Well, I'm happy for Jake."

"Cynthia, I'd hire you in a minute, if it weren't for the danger of it!"

"Oh. Don't worry. I could never work for a man like you!"

This set forth a howl from David. And, in the end, he hired her to keep an eye on the collector's house *at a distance*. And he kicked himself half the night.

The third day was uneventful. Both Jake and Cynthia reported a total lack of activity.

The next day was equally uneventful except that Cynthia said the collector had two visitors who arrived in a Mazda. Both men were dressed in suits and ties.

On Friday, Owen called David asking him to drop in at the front office when he got a chance. He found an immediate "chance" to get to Owen's Office. Josephine had him go right in.

"Hi, David. How're things going? Getting tired of it, yet?"

"No, sir! I love it here!"

"That's great. I wanted to see you because Frank Tubbs has been talking to me. He's telling me that a young friend of your's is staked out at Hornsby's place. And, a young lady friend of your's is, likewise, staked out at the collector's place. You do know that?"

The police were checking on Hornsby! They'd been right! Max would have had to put the finger on Hornsby. Then, he found he'd been called in for a message . . .

"David, the police believe it is very dangerous. Did you know that Hornsby bought a gun? I think you need to ask your friends to stop surveillance on these men."

"Yes, sir. I agree. I'll call both of them right away."

"David, I think you're going to have to trust the police in this. Yes, they think a transaction is in the making. They haven't given me any details, but they were grateful that you and your friends filled them in regarding Max. I did tell them I'd found out you had a claim to the letter. I think my messages went awry somehow. Neither the police, nor I, have perfect operations. We like to think we do, but it's not so. If I did, the letter would never have gone to Joe for evaluation.

"Now, I'd like to tell you something about the letter which may help. I know it's been bothering you. It has important historical significance and, if genuine, is worth a great deal of money." Here, he referred to his notebook. "It is contained in an old yellow cover envelope with a very faint message scribbled in cursive. I doubt if Max even noticed it. It is an old and very faint note written in script by someone named Mary McKay Kindle. I presume she was Julia McKay's daughter. Her note says that the Lincoln letter is to go to her granddaughter, MaryAnn Wickers."

Looking up, he said there was no connection to any family member which Max could furnish. "We couldn't touch it without proof of ownership."

David was elated. A Lincoln letter with *important historical significance*!

"Now, I will explain the historical significance of the letter when, or if, we can retrieve it. Will you go call off your friends, now?"

"Yes, sir!"

"Please call me Owen."

"Yes, sir, Mr. Owen . . . I mean . . ."

"Just go call them," laughed Owen.

In short order, he'd called both friends and said they could now *come in out of the cold.* "You've been ID'd by the cops!"

That evening they were all three gathered on David's porch. He suggested that they go over to Gin's house.

"I want to fill you all in on what I've found out from my boss."

They trooped into Gin's living room where she was dozing in front of the television. Taking the clicker, he turned down the loud volume which promptly awakened Gin.

"Hi, Gin. We came over to bring you up to date on the Lincoln letter. Owen, my boss, called me in this afternoon. He verified that the police were checking on Hornsby. We never mentioned Hornsby to the police, so Max had to have named his partner."

"Owen mentioned an illegal collector that Cynthia and he both thought might be an obvious buyer for the letter. The police have their eye on the collector, too. This brings me to the most exciting news. Owen says the Letter has *important historical significance* and has great value. Next, he says the outside envelope has a faint note on the backside."

Here, David pulled a piece of paper out of his shirt and read, "the enclosed letter is to be the property of my granddaughter, MaryAnn Vickers, and it's signed by Mary McKay Kindle."

"Ah! MaryAnn was my mother. I remember her telling me this!"

"Who was Mary McKay Kindle," asked Cynthia.

"She was the daughter of Julia James McKay. Her father was the Civil War hero, Taylor McKay. Oh! I hope you can get your letter back, David."

"Well, if he does, he's going to be a very wealthy man before he goes to college," laughed Jake.

"I'm glad for you, David. But, we still don't have the letter in hand. Will the cops get it?" Cynthia was clearly not satisfied. "Besides, I'm unemployed, again!"

Gin looked startled and, then, just smiled.

David was at a loss. They'd come so far it seemed, but Cynthia was right. There was still no letter. Would it get bumbled by the cops? He dreaded not *seeing* the letter.

CHAPTER 18

Break-In

SATURDAY MORNING THE THREE MET to take stock. David sat in his usual place on the porch swing with Cynthia.

"OK. We've made great progress. Now we know something about the letter itself. And, we know why Owen and Joe refused to deal with Max. We know that Hornsby has—or, almost certainly has—the Lincoln letter. We know he is trying to swing a deal with a collector, if he hasn't already. That's a lot more than we knew two weeks ago. But, Cynthia, here, is right. No letter in hand."

Cynthia frowned, saying, "David, I don't know how I got spotted. I saw no one out at the collector's place except for the two men who stopped to see him."

"I sure didn't see anyone at Hornsby's place," added Jake.

"Well," said David, "I'm not willing to take chances on my letter. It's a treasure. Imagine, a letter from Abraham Lincoln! So, what do you think the cops might do?"

"I've been thinking about that, without an answer," Cynthia said.

"I've no idea what cops do in situations like this," said Jake, shaking his head.

David spoke, "It worries me. Would they warn the collector and try to arrest Hornsby in the act of trying to sell stolen goods? Or, would they opt to tell Hornsby they'll go easy on him if he helps put the sting on the collector? Or, is there some other way?" David looked to Cynthia for a reaction.

After a long silence, Cynthia said, "David, I think we're getting out of our depth. I wish we could find a way to keep an eye on the collector. One way or another, he's going to have the transaction in his house or at a meeting place of his choosing. But, who knows for sure." She frowned and repeated herself. "Who knows for sure!"

Jake was quiet and offered no sign of having heard.

"Well, I want you both to know you remain on my payroll. So, go home and think this thing through. We probably don't have much time," David said, rising to his feet.

Monday morning brought news. When David walked in Josephine said Owen wanted to see him. Somehow, it sounded bad.

He entered the office saying "Yes, sir. You wanted to see me?"

"David, Detective Long called me last night at home. They arrested both Hornsby and the collector. They didn't find the letter. They will have to release both men in twenty-four hours."

David felt sick. No letter.

"David, I know how you feel. Go home for a couple of days. They may turn it up, yet."

"Thanks, sir. I would like to take a couple of days off."

He called Cynthia the minute he was out the door. She picked him up and they drove to Jake's farm.

"Here's my plan," David said, "it's going to be ticklish. They arrested both men at the dealer's place. No letter was found. It may be at Hornsby's place or in a locker someplace. I'd like to check Hornsby's house.

Now you two might not want any part of this. If so, don't hesitate to say. I am bribing you with an enormous salary of twelve dollars an hour. And, all you have to do is watch that I don't get caught," David smiled grimly. "This may be aiding and abetting, I suppose. I am going into Hornsby's house to make a search. It may take all day and all night but, then, I have to be out. And, I'm praying that the cops don't show up. So, I won't blame you if you want to bow out."

"Twelve dollars an hour . . . it's that bad, you think?" laughed Cynthia.

"Well, I can afford it!" grinned David.

"So, what's the plan," asked Jake.

"Cynthia, could you take the day shift and keep an eye open outside Hornsby's house?

I'm renting a van which you can park up the street a bit. If anyone shows up *near* to the house, call me on the cell."

"When do you want to start," asked Cynthia.

"Right now. Could you take the night shift, Jake?"

"No problem. Cynthia, when I relieve you, say about six-thirty, I'll drive by a couple of blocks and walk back to the van. Then, could you walk to your car? If there's a problem, have the parking lights on. OK?"

"Sure!"

Cynthia drove to a car rental place where David got the van he wanted. Then, she followed David to Hornsby's house and watched as he parked. She drove a couple of blocks down the street and walked back to the van. David made sure his flashlight and screwdriver were in his jacket pocket and walked across to Hornsby's house. He walked directly to the front door and rang the doorbell. After glancing around, he walked around the house to the back yard. He tried the back door. It was locked. He saw a ground level window to the basement and pulled the screwdriver from his pocket. He wedged the screwdriver between the window and sill and pried the window open. Turning on his flashlight he saw that he was immediately over a utility sink. He slipped through, stepped into the sink and hopped to the floor.

He was soon upstairs searching each room as thoroughly as he knew how. He tried to pass nothing up. He looked under carpets, behind pictures, under all surfaces, and in every single thing that opened. He searched all books and papers. When he arrived at the laundry room he looked in, under and around each appliance, checked among the towels and sheets and double checked. He tried to take nothing for granted.

By the time six-thirty arrived, he had reached the kitchen. He searched among the pots and pans, the dishes, in the appliances, in all the drawers, under the drawers, and on top of every surface. He was getting exhausted, but he kept to it.

He finally had the garage to search and tried to be careful with the flashlight as he found a stepladder and checked for a crawlspace. Finally, he was in the basement where he spent another two hours searching. He then marched upstairs and went from room to room studying each to see if there were anything he'd missed.

Calling it quits, he locked the basement window and went upstairs to the back door. Making sure it was locked behind him, he slipped around the house and was soon across the street and into the van.

"Any luck," asked Jake.

"None. I think it had already been searched by the police; I'm an amateur so why should I hope to find it if the cops couldn't. Where're you parked?"

"Down the street. Wonder what they did with his car," Jake said.

"They must have impounded it. Let's get home and get some rest. But I sure wish we could keep an eye on Hornsby's car. From the police impound to his driveway. He might have the letter stashed in it though the police have probably gone over it with a fine tooth comb!" David was nearly asleep as he dropped Jake at the old pickup.

When David woke up it was mid-afternoon. He called Jake asking if he might be able to go by the impound to check on Hornsby's car.

"Too late, pal," Jake laughed. I just followed him home from the impound. Remember, you're paying me twelve dollars an hour! Hey! Do I get night pay?"

"If you don't sleep on the job," said David.

"Well, he never paid a bit of attention to the car. Just drove it home and left it in the driveway."

"Where in hell has he put that Letter," groused David.

He called Cynthia and asked if she could pick him up at the car rental place. He had to get the van back.

Cynthia suggested that, perhaps, they were "back to a locker, again".

After Cynthia left him at home, he wearily went in for dinner. "Where is that Letter," he groaned.

CHAPTER 19

Hiding Place

DAVID AND HIS MOTHER MET with Owen, Wilbur and Josephine. He was given an in-depth briefing on the evaluation of the helmet and, in short, was offered two-hundred and twenty-nine thousand dollars. He accepted, and that amount was deposited to his bank account.

He presented a large check to his aunt Gin who tore it in several pieces saying, "David, that is *your* helmet. I gave it to you. And, I don't need money!"

David then met with Jake and Cynthia at her house. He drove his new car and parked behind Jake's pickup. Something had to be done about his Lincoln letter. He was sure that Hornsby had it somewhere.

"We've got to discover where he's hiding that letter. We know he had to be able to reach it quickly if he struck a deal with the collector. Is it still where it was when he was arrested? Did the cops tell them what they were looking for when they were arrested?

Or, does that even matter? Tell me where he might have it!" David looked at Jake and Cynthia in turn.

"Jake says he doesn't believe it's on the car anywhere. I think he's right.

This guy is real cute. He thinks he's a genius. I mean, he'd think of a Trojan Horse or something weird," David groused.

"Maybe he pulled an Abe Lincoln and carried it in his hat," laughed Cynthia.

"Was he wearing a hat when he was arrested," asked David.

"I suppose so. He wore a hat when he drove his car out of the police impound," exclaimed Jake.

"What kind of hat," asked David.

"A sort of business hat with a wide brim," Jake said.

"You mean a *fedora*," asked Cynthia.

"Yeah! A fedora."

"Why wouldn't they have looked in his hat?" Cynthia was puzzled.

"Maybe when they saw he was armed, they never thought about his hat," suggested David.

"Did he have a Concealed Weapons Permit," asked Cynthia.

"He must have one. If not, they'd be keeping him longer than twenty-four hours wouldn't they," asked Jake.

"My dad has a Concealed Weapons Permit. I'll check with him," smiled Cynthia as the boys looked at her. But, even if it were in his hat, where does that get us now?"

"See you two tomorrow. Meantime, here's a bonus for each of you," and he handed Jake and Cynthia each an envelope. Then, he left Cynthia's place driving his new car, an old Toyota sedan.

CHAPTER 20

———◆━━◆✕◆━━◆———

Letter Retrieved

OWEN HAD GIVEN HIM A week off as a bonus to the sale of his helmet. It was perfect timing.

The meeting on the porch availed little except profuse thanks. David had given five thousand dollars each to Jake and Cynthia.

"My folks just can't believe you did that, David," Cynthia said.

"Mine either," exclaimed Jake.

"OK, let's get down to business. How can we flush that letter out? Have you given thought to how he might have hidden the letter if not in the fedora?"

"Well, I'm for the fedora more than ever, said Cynthia. Did you ever see him wear a hat of any kind to school? Not that I ever noticed. No, the fedora is just too suspicious."

"He got released yesterday. I think we need to keep an eye on him. What's he doing as we speak," asked David. "Jake, could you drive over there now and, please, keep out of sight! I'll be over and let you head home before long. But, if he leaves before I get there, follow him, and for Pete's sake, *call me!*"

"You've got it," and Jake was walking out to his truck.

David thought for a moment and then asked Cynthia if she could keep an eye on the collector's place. She nodded and headed for her car. "And call if anything happens," David yelled.

David had a curious feeling. Things felt like they were headed for a conclusion of some sort. It was queer. He decided he would drive to Hornsby's house and talk to Jake. A few minutes minutes later his cell rang. Cynthia said the two men she'd seen before had just left the collector's house.

David had pulled to the curb. He knew that they were in way over their heads. But where were the cops! Was he risking his friends lives? He sat and brooded. Was it really worth pursuing? He started the car after thinking it all over and resumed the drive to Hornsby's house.

He was only a block away when the cell rang again. It was Jake. "Two guys like the ones Cynthia told us about just drove up. Looks like they're going in."

"I'm just about there, and here's what I want. Follow them if they leave. I'll stay with Hornsby. But, Jake, take no chances. Stay way back. If you lose them, so be it. We're not cops."

In minutes he pulled up behind Jake's pickup. Before he could open his door to talk to Jake, the two men walked out of Hornsby's house. Jake followed their car down the street leaving David to watch the house.

It was a very curious David . . . was Hornsby OK? Or, was he lying on the floor inside bleeding to death? His answer came on the heels of these thoughts.

Hornsby came out wearing the fedora and carrying a briefcase. He drove off in a hurry. David tried to keep up without being noticed but it proved difficult. Too, he'd be recognized if he got too close. It had become a semi rural area with few commercial buildings scattered among fields.

Suddenly there was a tremendous crash. At first, he thought Hornsby's car had exploded as dust flew everywhere. When he'd pulled to the side of the road he saw that Hornsby had broadsided a semi truck and trailor. He was lying half in and half out of the smashed car. The truck driver was bent over apparently taking the teacher's pulse.

"I've called 911. There's help on the way," he said, not looking up at David. No one else was in sight. David saw the fedora on the crumpled dash and casually reached over and picked it up. He ran his fingers around the inside of the hat and felt an envelope tucked inside. When he looked he could see nothing. He decided the best thing was to get the hat to his car where he could check it out.

"How's he doing," David asked the truck driver who was clearly shaken.

"Can't feel a pulse," gulped the man whose face had become pale.

David returned to his car and quickly felt the envelope. He was able to pull the dark fabric away revealing an old yellow envelope. He saw faint penciled writing on the backside of the envelope and set it on the car seat.

Something prompted him to return to the wrecked car. He heard a siren in the distance and moving to the wrecked car, dropped the hat on the seat. He retrieved the briefcase from the floorboard and carried it back to the Toyota just as the red emergency truck arrived with a police car behind.

David didn't want to remain, but a policeman was already approaching his car. "Did you see this happen?"

"No sir. I was a block away and just saw an explosion of dust. How is he?" The cop shrugged and walked back to the wrecked car. The truck driver was sitting on the curb with his head in his hands.

David lifted the briefcase up on the seat and saw it was a combination lock. When he touched the button it opened revealing a handgun. There was nothing else.

He closed the lid and slid the briefcase into the back floorboard. It was too late to return the briefcase. Too, he was reluctant to have his name appear as a witness on the accident report along with Mr. Hornsby's. He wanted out of here. Especially he wanted that handgun out of his car.

His mind was made up for him when he saw a car with two men pull up at the wreck site. They were shortly joined by Jake. The old pickup pulled up behind David.

He walked back to the door of Jake's truck saying, "I have it. I got his hat and the yellow envelope was in it! What are those two doing here? They must have a bug in his car or something."

"Ya got me, Dave. Quite an accident! How is he?"

"I'm not sure he's alive." David was staring at the car with the two men. They both had walked around Hornsby's car looking inside. The emergency workers had Hornsby on a stretcher and were pushing needles into him while fitting a breathing apparatus to his face.

The two men were looking at Jake and David. David told Jake to take off. In a minute Jake turned the old Ford in a U-turn going away from the accident.

David set the yellow envelope on the seat beside him and started the car. The policeman was talking to the truck driver and making notes on a clipboard.

David turned the old car into a U-turn and followed Jake. Immediately the two men were turning behind him. Why were they following, David wondered. Were they the police? David knew he'd slipped up somewhere. They couldn't be police. Cynthia had seen them more than once entering and leaving the collector's house. These guys were the collector's men.

CHAPTER 21

Letter Lost

D AVID CAME TO A STOP behind a line of cars at a stoplight. Before he knew it a man had opened the passenger door and pointed a very large and scary gun at him.

"Just relax, son. This won't hurt a bit." He reached over and picked up the yellow envelope. "This is all I need. Have a great day." He laughed as he slammed the car door.

David was stunned. It had happened so fast. He'd been held up by a man with a gun, and his letter was gone already. He watched helplessly as their car swung out of the traffic and turned back. Cars were already honking at him. He managed to swing the car around into a U-turn, but the two men were nowhere to be seen.

He headed towards the collector's house and called Cynthia. He wanted to know if the two men appeared there. He was sure they would.

When he arrived Cynthia had not seen the two men. David was staggered. He'd had it in his hands . . . Now, he had no idea what to do.

"Cynthia, I don't dare leave this place without someone to watch for those men. Or, maybe the collector is going somewhere to pick it up. What do you think?"

She couldn't think of anything else to do, either. David called Jake and found he was just down the block. He told him about losing the letter at gunpoint. He wanted both Cynthia and Jake to know how dangerous this had become. And they were not police with professional training. Why weren't the cops doing this!

"If the collector leaves, follow him, Jake." Jake nodded as David returned to Cynthia;s car. He climbed in and told her about the crash of Hornsby's car. He told her how right she had been about the hat. He'd had the Lincoln Letter for all of ten minutes before giving it up at gunpoint.

"If you get near those two men be very careful. Just drive away! I still don't know how they knew me or that I had the Letter. But they're armed, and they don't fool around!" With that he walked back to the old Toyota.

The house door opened and a man went to a silver car in the driveway. None of them had seen the collector. Was this him? David shook his head in frustration. Jake had pulled out and was a good half block in back of the silver car. After a few seconds of wondering what he should do, he pulled out and followed Jake.

They were driving for thirty minutes before David saw the silver car make a a swift U-turn just as the two men had done after holding him up. David took the next right turn and sped around the block in hopes of seeing the silver car. He felt great relief to see the silver car just ahead and making a right turn.

He raced to the corner in time to see the silver car swing into a motel. Slowing to a crawl he approached the motel and parked on the street. He felt in the back and pulled Hornsby's briefcase into the front seat, opened it to view the handgun, shook his head and closed the case.

He could see nothing of the silver car. He walked down the street to where he could see cars parked behind the units. He walked between shrubs and newly planted trees until he was on a sidewalk circling the units.

There was the silver car. It was parked beside the Mazda. Somehow he knew this might be his last chance to get the Letter. But, what to do?

He slowly walked behind the parked cars until he was behind the silver car. He crouched down and slid up to the driver's door. It was unlocked. He opened the door slowly reached to the dash near his head and pulled open the plastic door to the fuses. He pulled all the fuses and closed the small door. Then, he reached up under the dash and felt a bundle of wires. He pulled as hard as he could. There was no noise. He closed the car door until he heard a click.

CHAPTER 22

The Letter

H E WAS MOVING BACK TO the rear of the car when a motel door opened in front of the right headlight, and he heard voices of men talking.

David moved swiftly on hands and knees back and around the car parked on the left side of the silver car. That car looked like the ones driven by the two men. He managed to squeeze between two cars just down the line which was very lucky since there were only six cars parked in front of the units.

Car doors opened and closed, and the two men were backing out and driving away. David heaved a sigh of relief as the silver car remained silent and unmoving. The car door opened and the man stood looking at it suspiciously.

David lowered his head. He listened as footsteps sounded on the sidewalk coming towards David and the parked cars.

David slowly moved behind the car nearest to the silver car. He remained on his knees. The footsteps continued on down the walk and around the units towards the office.

David walked around the silver car to the passenger side. He looked into the car. Nothing to see. Then he saw the briefcase on the floor on the passenger side. In a sort of desparation, he opened the driver's door and reached in pulling the briefcase onto the driver's seat. He clicked the latch. He was stunned! There lay the old yellow envelope. He had it and ran quickly around the unit the way he had entered. He glanced toward the office but saw nothing. He got to the Toyota and drove off.

He had the Lincoln Letter! He'd not give it up again!

CHAPTER 23

Evaluation

H E CALLED CYNTHIA AND JAKE asking them to meet him at "AA Rare Documents and Antiquities".

The three were soon on the elevator and were greeted by Jo.

"Jo, I have an Abraham Lincoln Letter which I wish to have evaluated. It's not for sale, however."

Jo smiled and called Owen. He quickly appeared and motioned the three through the swinging gates.

"Folks, let's go into my office and take a seat. So, you have your letter." He smiled as David handed him the old yellow envelope.

"Yes. That looks like what Max brought us. Dave who are your friends? Not the ones who got found out for being on surveilance?"

"I'm afraid so, sir. This lady is Cynthia White, my girlfriend, and this is Jake Taylor. Without them I wouldn't have the Letter."

"Are you in any way in danger," asked Owen as he stood and shook hands with Cynthia and Jake.

"I'm afraid I just don't know. I got the Letter from the collector . . . the guy they arrested with Hornsby. I think Hornsby may be dead. He was in a bad car accident," David said without going into detail.

"David, would you mind if I talked with Frank or Sam at the police department? I'd hate to see harm come to any of you. Men like this can be very dangerous."

"Fine with me. To tell the truth I'd feel relief. We may well need police protection."

Owen immediately had Jo call the department and Owen was talking to Frank. After he hung up, he asked if they'd mind waiting until Frank and Sam arrived. They agreed. At Owen's suggestion, David took them for a guided tour.

He especially was anxious for them to meet Will who'd worked on the helmet, and Joe, who would work on the Lincoln Letter. Will was his usual vivacious self and greatly entertained the trio.

When they entered Joe's office he lookd up and smiled. "So, Owen says you've brought the Lincoln letter back for another viewing," he said, standing and offering chairs.

"Yes, sir. It's long overdue. I'm awfully glad that you're working on it!" He quickly introduced his friends making sure they received due credit for rescuing the Letter.

Soon they were back in the front office where they were met by Owen, Frank and Sam.

Frank looked at them shaking his head. "Which one of those crooks had the letter?"

"Hornsby had it", David smiled.

"Where in hell did he have it? We searched him and that car inch by inch."

"Well, Cynthia figured that out. He had it in his fedora."

"His *what?*"

"His hat. He had it in his hat," David grinned.

"How the devil did you get ahold of it?"

And, so, David told them about the accident and of being held up by the two men. By the time he'd finished his tale about the motel and getting the letter, Frank was seated and looking worried.

"You do realize that the three of you are known to those men. And, you already know how dangerous they are. Sam will follow you to the station. I think we may need to protect your families, too." But, he gave no lecture regarding their activities.

As they were leaving, Owen walked beside David and asked, "Did you read the letter?"

"Yes, sir. I did. And I see why it has historical significance. I'll be glad to loan it to the University for a time *after I am done with my work*, but I want the letter back. I will write a dissertation and, eventually, a book. So, I will get legal help to keep this letter mine until I get my publications completed. Then, I'll hang it in our home for Mom and Aunt Gin."

CHAPTER 24

———◆◆※◆◆———

Protection

The police called in Cynthia's parents, Jake's Dad and David's Mom. They received a stern lecture about the danger they might be in.

After Cynthia's Mother was thoroughly frightened, they were excused in company of an officer who would stay at the White residence until the police felt there was no longer a danger. The police were vague about when, or why, that might be.

It seemed to David that nothing would come from the police talking to the collector. He'd simply deny everything. And, on the long-shot of their finding the two men who worked for him, it would probably be much the same.

Jake's dad declined protection. They lived with Bob and out in the country. "No one in his right mind would try to bother us. We'd see them coming a mile away."

And, so, David and his Mother had the dubious privilege of a live-in female officer. She would accompany Mrs. Thornton to work before dropping David off at the Documents firm.

Then, at four, she'd pick up Mrs. Thornton before picking David up and bringing them home. She'd spend the night and resume the same routine next day. After four days she'd be relieved by another officer.

David admitted to Jake that she was a beautiful young officer who looked very attractive in her uniform. "And, yes, she's armed but easy going," David told his friend. The officer who relieved her was just the opposite. She hardly allowed either his Mother or himself out of her sight.

Cynthia called complaining of absolute boredom. Her Mother continued to be angry with David, but "Dad just laughs and carries his concealed gun."

"Well, I can't blame your Mom. Looking back, I think I wouldn't do anything that'd put you in danger. I just wouldn't do that again! But I can't see what the collector or his men could gain by bothering any of us, now. Oh! Did you hear that Hornsby died at the scene of the accident?"

The days passed without incident until Frank came out one Saturday morning saying they were calling protection off. They'd talked to the collector, but hadn't located the other two men.

It felt good to have Cynthia and Jake back on the front porch. They all trooped over to Gin's and ate pie. They related all the details of the long pursuit of the Letter. David took this opportunity to explain the historical significance of the Letter.

CHAPTER 25

Cynthia

THE SUMMER WAS COMING TO a close, and the three friends found themselves enrolling together at the local university.

David received a going-away party in which Owen presented an award for Meritorious Service. He looked around the room and was choked up. He'd made many friends here, and almost wished it were next summer.

He had a final meeting with Owen in which he asked a final favor. Owen thought about it briefly and agreed.

Then, he left the large building and made his way to his old car.

The weeks passed and cold weather moved in as the three friends found themselves getting more involved with their studies.

One dark afternoon, David left his Math class and headed toward his car. As he opened the car door, dumping his books on the seat, he felt something hard in his back.

"Yes, it's a gun. Just come with me." He couldn't see who it was but backed away from the car. "Now, I want no foolishness. We have your girl friend, so do just as I tell you."

David felt a sharp fear hit him in the solar plexis. My God! What did they want? It couldn't be the Letter. It was here at the University being studied by history professors. He wasn't even sure he knew where it was stored. It had even made the national news.

He was put into the rear seat of a car beside another man. Both men looked familiar, and he felt he was back with old acquaintances.

The car sped onto a freeway and was soon out of town. It was about time for cars to have lights on.

"Is Cynthia . . ."

"Shut up!"

David shut up. He was strangled with fear. Was Cynthia OK?

Befoe long the car slowed and turned off onto a side road leading into a small rural community. Soon it pulled off onto a gravel road. The driver went slowly for about two miles before turning down a long lane. They parked in front of an old farmhouse.

The familiar silver car was parked in front of the farmhouse. David was pulled out and shoved towards the front door of the farmhouse. The door opened and he saw the collector.

"Well, come on in. It's been a while. Couldn't leave well enough alone, could you?" The man was not at all friendly.

"As you know, I am Mr. Saterous. It's time we met."

"You were very clever, David. I was careless at the motel. Very careless. I'm usually not. But, I'll come right to the point. I want that letter . . . nothing more and nothing less.

Vick, here, will drive you into the University. I'll give you three hours to get it and walk back through that door and hand it to me. No delay. Understood?"

"Yes. Where's Cynthia. I want to see her."

"If you fail to return with letter in hand, Cynthia will never be seen again. Hurry. Your time is running out. Vick won't waste time."

He turned and almost ran out to the car. Vick had him sit in front of the black Mazda. They weren't worried about him now. It was a mistake.

CHAPTER 26

The Offensive

D AVID HAD FORMED HIS PLAN weeks earlier. He directed Vick to his old Toyota still parked at the University. He said he kept a key in his car which he needed in order to get to the letter at the University. Vick had no hesitation and drove directly to the Toyota.

David pulled the briefcase from the back seat, opened it and pulled the .45 automatic out and behind his thigh. He returned to the Mazda where Vick waited unconcerned. Vick started the car as David slumped in the passenger seat. Vick was turning the car into the street when he felt the muzzle of the gun at his temple. Vick almost froze and turned just in time to avoid going into the oncoming lane.

In only minutes Frank and another police car were on the scene and Vick was taken into custody.

"O-K, David. I have a swat team on the way; they'll follow the Mazda he brought you in. I'll drive and you will be in the seat beside me so we don't get lost. When we get there, you will go to the swat team's vehicle. Now, I need that weapon you have."

The long hours of training given by Mr. White had made it easy thought David. He'd never shot a gun before the training he'd received from Mr. White.

They slowed and stopped on the gravel road just outside the small community. They sat in the dark watching the clock on the dash. They had thirty-five minutes left. The collector would be getting jumpy, thought David. It probably shouldn't have taken this much time. But, the swat team was right behind them.

There was a quick briefing. "There are two of them that we know of, armed. Saterous expects David and Vick to walk through that door. He'll expect David and Vick. Instead, he gets Captain Terry and his swat team."

There was no car at the farmhouse. The lights had been turned off. David's heart was thumping in alarm. He ran into the farmhouse. The lights revealed an empty house. He saw a letter on the table dramatically held in place with a hunting knife blade stuck into the wood.

The letter was short and to the point. "Leave the document in the mailbox at my house. Nothing undue, or Cynthia won't survive."

"What now," asked David. He felt he should have foreseen this.

CHAPTER 27

Found

D AVID WAS PERMITTED TO RIDE with Frank as the swat team returned to the city and made its way to the Saterous residence. No one was there.

Now there would be a massive manhunt as it involved a kidnapping. David was sick. Why had they trusted the police, especially when Cynthia's life was at stake. He sat in his car in the dark in deep thought. Was there anything he could do. Then, his cell phone rang. It was Saterous.

"David. I want the letter put into my hands immediately. I am parked behind you. I have Cynthia with me. Don't think of calling anyone. Just keep talking to me and get out of your car. Walk back towards me. When you hand me the letter, I'll release your girl friend.

And, thankfully, he did.

The next day David stopped to see Owen. He reported that the Collector had bought the reproduction. This would not be the end, he knew. Before long the Collector would find that the real Lincoln Letter was not the one he possessed. David wouldn't have much time. Meanwhile, the police put the University on alert that no publicity about the letter could be used until Saterous was apprehended.

CHAPTER 28

Threats

ONE EVENING AS DAVID WAS studying math his cell phone rang. He opened the cell to hear the voice of the collector. He simply said, "You should have believed me," and the phone went dead.

Why hadn't the police been able to find Saterous?

David called Jake and asked him to come into town. Then, he called Cynthia who quickly joined them. David explained the problem. The call was meant to make them suffer.

"Jake, could you take Cynthia to that seminar you've been wanting to attend?"

"You're kidding! The one in Victoria?"

"That's the one. You'd be gone a week. Could this be worked out with your professors?"

"This is going to be expensive, Dave."

"No problem. It's just money."

Owen called Officer Frank and asked that police protection be afforded to David's mother and aunt and to Cynthia's parents. Jake's Dad and Uncle wanted none as they were confident of safety on their farm.

And so, Cynthia and Jake were off to Victoria and out of harms way. David knew Saterous had to be stopped. But what about his henchman? Time to see where the remaining snake, or snakes, had a den. Vick had been apprehened the night Saterous had abducted Cynthia.

For the next several nights he camped out in a rented travel trailer parked up the street from the collector's empty house. He finally saw a man arrive one night and figured time might be running out. He walked across the street in the darkness and stuck a device under the rear bumper as he'd been instructed. He went back to the trailer and got in the small car which had been hitched behind. He turned a switch and received the beeps. He sat back and waited. Finally, the car left the driveway. Why had this guy come to an empty house?

He followed the vehicle at a safe distance keeping up with the beeps. Before long the vehicle stopped. David found it with ease. It was parked at an apartment house. He was able to find the apartment as the man was entering. Lights came on. He quietly climbed the stairs and made sure he had the apartment number. Then, he sat in his car until the man departed. It was eleven the next morning. He walked across the street and climbed the stairs. He was soon in the apartment. The credit card worked on opening the door just as he'd been shown. That Mr. White sure knew lots of valuable stuff. He quickly hunted up a pile of bills and got the cell number. The bills had been sent to Holland Jones.

That evening he gave it a try. He dialed the cell phone number. A familaar voice answered. He said nothing and hung up. A few hours later he phoned again. This time the man said nothing. David also said nothing and hung up.

In the middle of the night, he drove back to the apartment and taped a letter to the front door. Then, he drove to the collector's house. He was now very familiar with the house.

In the dark, he made his way across the street and was out of sight in seconds.

It was done. It'd be a firm message which could not be misunderstood by the collector or his hirling, Mr. Holland Jones.

CHAPTER 29

<hr />

The News

CYNTHIA AND JAKE ARRIVED AT the airport early the next morning, and David was there to pick them up. Cynthia was quickly in David's arms saying how worried she'd been.

"Nothing to worry about."

"Oh, I'll always be a nervous wreck with that viper around!" Cynthia shook her fist in the air.

"Dave," said Jake, "have you got anything to tell us?"

"Well, the last henchman has left town. I think for good."

"How do you know," asked Cynthia.

"I called him this morning, and he was already pretty far south. He said he was done with this part of the country."

"We'll want to hear the full story. Oh, Victoria was wonderful!" Cynthia hung on David's arm as they picked up the luggage.

Jake had already picked up a newspaper. He was reading a front page story about a residential house which had mysteriously blown up. A gas leak was suspected.

Just below this story was a smaller headline about a Lincoln letter recently recovered and verified as genuine. Now, "one of the great mysteries of the Civil War seemed to be on the verge of being solved only awaiting the publications of Mr. David Thornton, owner of the lettter."

CHAPTER 30

◆━❖━◆

Shadows

DAVID CONTINUED WITH HIS STUDIES but worried. He tried to keep a close eye on Cynthia but felt it was nearly impossible. Something was wrong. There was no sign of Saterous. Where was he?

Months went by and spring had arrived. The attack came at a most unexpected moment. He and Jake were fishing with Bob on a Sunday afternoon. Bob, as usual, had caught several nice fish and released them. David and Jake had watched him from the bank. He was a master with the fly rod and had the perfect flies as he landed fish after fish only to release them.

Tiring of watching the master, they walked off upstream hoping to catch a few to take home. David passed Jake at a nice hole as Jake said "Luck, Dave." "You, too," David said, passing on upstream for a favorite hole. It was just around a sharp bend in the river.

He had made only one cast when he heard the shot. At first he wasn't sure where it had come from. It sounded as if the shot had come from behind him and up the bank from the river. Suddenly he dropped the rod and began running. As he neared the pool he couldn't see Jake. He screamed "Jake!" There was no answer. Then, he saw the white pullover under the fishing vest. Jake was lying on the ground. The shirt was turning red.

Bob came up and dropped to his knees beside David. Jake was alive. His breathing was shallow as David called 911 and summoned help. David watched as Bob tightened a piece of his cotton shirt around the shoulder. Jake's rod remained in his hand, the fly floating somewhere near the shore.

How much time passed he didn't know. He'd ran back to the truck and met the ambulance at the blacktop. Jake was now in the hands of the medics. After sharp words, the medics allowed David to accompany them in the ambulance.

Bob paid little attention to the young Sheriff's deputies. One suggested it was probably just a hunting accident. Bob looked disbelieving and said "Right. Must be deer season!" Of course, it wasn't.

The young man flushed and said "OK. But some kid could have just been shooting."

Bob had no comment and hurried off to see Jake's parents. He'd have to take them to the hospital.

Jake's dad was almost without emotion. His mom was frightened. David and Bob were affected differently. They were angry. Deeply, coldly angry. When Jake opened his eyes he looked up to see his dad and mom, Uncle Bob and David. Moments later, Cynthia arrived.

The doctors said he'd make it.

CHAPTER 31

Terry

D AVID MET WITH CYNTHIA'S PARENTS. They'd hire a bodyguard for Cynthia until school was out. Then, she'd go to Oregon to live with relatives for the summer. David heaved a sigh of relief. She'd live in a remote area away from Portland. She'd be safe. He hoped.

Bob and David met to discuss a plan of action. Something had to be done. David would research Saterous' family. Did he have family here in the city? What was his background? Was he independently wealthy? Had he inherited his wealth? Where did he bank? The questions were endless. If the police had a record on him, they weren't sharing it.

Clearly the man was mentally and criminally insane. After all that had happened, and even considering that he was wanted, his mind seemed devoted to one thing—getting the Lincoln letter.

David would work on the Internet trying to track Saterous. Was his collection very large? Where was it kept? Was it still there? The questions just kept piling up.

He met with Bob each week to compare notes. Bob had discovered that the Saterous family was very wealthy living on estates near Chicago. Bob took nothing for granted. He'd talked to anyone he could find in the old neighborhood around the exploded house. He went to each business within two miles of the old residence. He'd located two firms where Saterous had had transactions. One was a cleaners and the other was a local bank though the account had been closed.

The bank was Bob's choice for finding out more about Saterous. Where had the account been transferred, if it had been transferred?

"Dave, could you get any information about him on the Internet? I mean could you get into the bank's records?"

"I don't think I could do more than get into trouble. But, there's a guy at the University who might be able to help." He was already kicking himself for not having talked to Terry. That guy could do anything with a computer. The question was would he be willing?

"How's Jake doing? I was up to see him yesterday, and he was talking about a release to go home."

"Yeah. That's what his folks were told. He's getting better. I told him what we're doing."

Bob had got a lead from some court records. Years before Saterous had been arrested in Chicago for stealing from a museum. So, Bob was off to Chicago.

David met with Terry and was frank about what he wanted and why. Terry had met Jake but hadn't really known him. He knew David because of the Lincoln Letter. Nearly everyone at the University had at least heard of him and his Lincoln Letter.

Terry was shocked as David told him the entire story. He agreed to try to access bank records on Saterous.

"I'll promise nothing. But, I'll give it a try. I just don't want to end up in jail."

"No. That's the last place I want to see you, Terry. Be careful. If it gets touch and go . . . if you think you might get caught, drop it."

"I have a few other ideas. I'll try to find time. Do you have a first name for Saterous?"

"Yeah. Bob said his first name is *Conrad.*"

"Conrad Saterous. I'll do the best I can and get back to you."

CHAPTER 32

Owen

DAVID HEADED BACK ACROSS CAMPUS for a class feeling he'd made some progress. Still, he knew he was missing something. It was driving him nuts. It nagged him but studies seemed to interfere by dredging his memory.

He was getting into his car when it came to him. He headed downtown. Soon he was being greeted by Josephine.

"Hi. Is Owen in," he asked, as he sat at Josephine's desk.

"He'll be back in just a minute. He's down talking to one of the specialists. How's school going?"

"It's going great, Jo. Been a good year except for Jake. That's turned it pretty grey.

But, his dad has been able to arrange for him to study while he's in the hospital."

"I need to talk to Owen about the counterfeit letter. I wonder if Saterous could have discovered that letter was counterfeit on his own?"

"Oh. He'd had to have professional help on that. Saterous is really an amateur collector. I'm surprised he'd even have had it checked out. But, he probably took it to Pearson."

"Who's Pearson?"

"He's got a small business evaluating documents and other stuff. He's got an equally small reputation in the field. He's been suspected of working on stolen stuff. I don't think he buys much, but who knows. You can check with Owen. He'll know much more than I do."

On cue, Owen came in and, seeing David, grinned saying, "Glad to see you can't stay away!"

"Yes, sir. My favorite place." David had stood and was shaking Owen's outstretched hand.

"Come on in," said Owen, leading the way to his office. "I've been wanting to talk to you. School ends soon, and I have been thinking of a different job for you. Maybe starting an internship with the specialists. I thought we might rotate you from specialist to specialist. How'd you feel about that? I mean, it would just be for the summer. Wouldn't interfere with school."

"Wow! That would be great. I can't think of anything I'd rather do." David felt better than he had since Jake had been shot.

"Great! We'll get you started with Will. So, what brings you here today?"

He told Owen what he'd said to Josephine and received the same answer.

"Now, Pearson has a shady reputation, but he'd be able to tell if the letter were a counterfeit. Not sure why it would have taken weeks to have it confirmed. But, maybe Saterous hadn't thought of it sooner. Who knows?"

"Would you know where Saterous lives?"

"No. But, he comes from a wealthy family. They have a good reputation, too. Why are you trying to find him, David?"

"Because Jake nearly died. And, I think Cynthia is in danger."

"Be careful, David. Jake has been bad enough."

CHAPTER 33

Terry Digs

S CHOOL ENDED, AND DAVID HAD two weeks before his intern program would begin. He'd introduced Terry and Bob. Terry related a concise biography of Saterous.

"Basically, Saterous is unhinged. At sixteen, he was institutionalized for three years. He had been arrested for theft of a valuable article from a Chicago museum. He is paranoid. He is obsessed with rare and valuable objects. He comes from a very wealthy family. After his release from the mental institution he soon came into his inheritance. He considers himself a genius. He believes that the cops are after him. He is determined to never again be arrested or go back to the mental hospital. He has a tendency to violence."

Bob looked at him and said, "How in hell did you get all that?"

"From his psychologist's file. It's on a computer file."

"Amazing! Totally amazing." Bob decided he liked this guy.

"I got a call from Joe White, David said. He wants to work with us. Says he fed up with having to keep a close eye on his daughter and worrying all the time. Besides, he says he's given all of us training and wants to see how we're doing."

"Can't blame him, Bob said, sounding just as angry as Joe White had sounded.

"By the way, I have an address near Chicago for Saterous," Terry said.

"Well, I'll just run up there and see what it looks like," Bob announced.

"You'll find a mansion. He probably keeps his treasures there, but he is seldom seen there. Apparently, he has a few 'safe' houses here and there," Terry said.

Bob just shook his head saying, "All of that from a computer!"

CHAPTER 34

At The River

BOB SUGGESTED A TRIP OUT to the river. Neither of them had been there since Jake was shot. Bob parked Jake's old pickup in their usual parking place and opened the tailgate where he sat. David hopped up beside him.

"Dave, I just want to know what your plans are. And what do you think I ought to do."

"I'm not sure. I've thought about it, of course. It's just so full of shadows. Who is the shooter? Where is Conrad Saterous? I'm worried about Cynthia. My God, what if they harm her? He couldn't bring himself to say' *Or, worse*. I've been worried about your expenses. Do you need any money? I can help."

"No. Ben and I have enough. As you know Jake's mom is an invalid, and Ben has to be with her almost constantly. I think I could work with Joe White. We get along pretty well. We've been talking about finding Saterous. He's been the heart of this whole ugly thing." Bob tugged on his mustache and looked at David.

"OK. I'll try to track the shooter. If I get a lead, I'll call you," David said, as he slid off the tailgate.

"One more thing, Dave. The reason I wanted to come out here . . . don't let this change us. Jake would hate that. When it's all over I want us three to come out here and fish again." Dave looked at Bob without speaking and nodded his head.

"Don't let it get to you, Dave. We'll get him."

CHAPTER 35

Brush With Death

CYNTHIA WAS OFF THE CURB and glanced at a rapidly approaching car. The bodyguard was a brawny young man with a head on his shoulders. He saw the oncoming car and had his hand on Cynthia bicep. At the last minute, he knew. The car wasn't going to stop.

Barely in time he pulled her back toward the curbing. The driver had swerved thinking they'd choose to rush on across, the natural thing to do. He'd been out- guessed. As it was the fender had brushed Cynthia's dress. Both knew it was no accident. Neither had seen the driver behind the tinted glass.

As instructed, the young bodyguard immediately called Joe White. Joe wasted no time.

Professors would forward exams to the White residence. They would be resent to Oregon where Cynthia would be with a relative. The relative would whisk Cynthia away from the Portland International Airport and fly her in her small plane to a location not too far away. Then, Joe called David and said he was meeting with the police. Would Dave join him.

The meeting came to little. Neither Cynthia or the bodyguard had seen the driver. What was the license number? They hadn't seen it. Of course the police knew about her alleged abduction the previous fall. But, there was just nothing to go on. One of the detectives suggested that Mr. White take precautions if he really believed that his daughter was in danger. White already had.

CHAPTER 36

Oregon

A week later, David had finished his last exam. In two weeks, he'd begin his intern- ship. He boarded a flight going to Salt Lake. He'd change planes there and fly on to Portland where Cynthia and her aunt would be waiting. Mom and Gin insisted on taking him to the airport.

As promised, he was met by Cynthia and her Aunt Beatrice. After hugs, they proceeded to the small single-engine aircraft. Aunt Beatrice was an accomplished pilot and soon had them off the runway and headed up the Willamette River. The country was beautiful with snow-capped Mt. Hood, Jefferson and the Cascades stretching down the length of the State.

In just a bit over thirty minutes, Aunt Beatrice put the small plane down on a country strip at a place she called "Mulino". She parked and tied the plane down and took them to a sedan parked nearby.

Cynthia couldn't stop talking about the beautiful country. She'd fallen in love with Oregon. "Oh! Wait till we show you the Columbia Gorge! There's just no end of beautiful nature here."

A few hours later they were driving into a place called "Sweet Home". It was truly beautiful with timbered mountains on the east and running north and south as far as the eye could see. Aunt Beatrice had her home here but elected to have lunch in a restaurant.

Then, they dropped her off at home and drove off to see the sights.

"Cyn, I'm confused. Why does your aunt use a landing place so far away from Sweet Home?"

Cynthia laughed. "She's practicing deception. She would ordinarily land her plane here but files her flight plan to Molino to misdirect anyone who may be trying to follow."

Cynthia moved off the main highway and drove to a state maintained trail system and parked. Then, she enthusiastically marched off on a trail with David following. After half an hour, David called a halt to catch his breath. It was then that the shot came.

At first, he thought he'd just been kicked. It was when he realized he was flat on his back that he saw the blood. He'd been shot! The blood was coming out just below his left shoulder.

Cynthia was absolutely cool. She made sure they moved quickly with David nearly dragged into the brush off the trail. She ripped his shirt into strips and tightly bound the wound going above his shoulder and under his armpit. It staunched the flow of blood. By now, it hurt like hell, and he felt faint.

As soon as the wound was bound up she pulled a small .380 handgun from her pocket and fired three shots into the air.

They remained with David stretched on his back for nearly an hour. No one had come even after several more shots.

So, with Cynthia's help, he managed to stand. After a grueling two hours, they reached the car. And, in minutes, he was in an emergency room receiving aid. The police came. They could tell little. They'd hiked up the trail and never saw the shooter. Yes, she had a Concealed Weapon Permit for the .380.

CHAPTER 37

Identified

D AVID SPENT THE NEXT TWO days in a hospital bed and then successfully fought his way to a discharge. Cynthia insisted on flying with him back home.

"Cynthia, I'm uncomfortable leaving you in Oregon *and* in letting you return home. What are we to do? Obviously, they know where you live here. But, I would bet quite a large sum that the shooter's going to be on the plane with us."

"What!" Cynthia had turned pale.

"Oh. He'll have to be on the plane. How else could he know where we'll be going? No. His job is simple. Keep track of us. Kill us if he can. He's made at least two attempts. I think he's serious."

He'd booked the first two seats in First Class and sat on the isle. He carefully studied each figure that boarded the plane. Then, after they'd been in the air for an hour he excused himself and walked back and opened the curtain into coach. He studied the first two rows. One man on the right and seated by the window was sleeping with a pillow pulled over his face. That's got to be him, thought David. Small guy. Blue suit. Then, he returned to his seat.

"What was that all about," asked Cynthia.

He quietly told her what he'd been up to.

"Why just the first *two* rows?"

"We change planes in Salt Lake. He has to keep on our heels. No. There's no doubt in my mind. That's him. With this bum arm in a sling, he's not afraid of me. He just has to keep track."

In Salt Lake they disembarked. David stood just outside the aircraft as passengers came down the stairs from it and picked up their luggage from a large cart. The small man in the blue suit had not come off the aircraft. David ran up the stairs saying, "Left my carry-on in the cabin." He rushed into First Class, and there stood the man in the blue suit. He was almost tiny. So, he was face to face, finally, with the shooter. Somehow, *he knew.*

He pointed the cell phone and clicked the picture. "This isn't over, yet. But, you're a marked man," he said. Then, he turned and left the cabin. The little man hadn't said a word.

CHAPTER 38

Taken

H E'D NOT FORGET THAT FACE, picture or no. Not ever. But he
wanted the picture downloaded and enlarged for the benefit of
Bob, Joe and Terry. He finally decided to show the picture to Cynthia.
Pray God she'd never see that face again.

That evening Cynthia sat with her Dad, Bob and Terry. She'd not
met Terry and was introduced. Mrs. White sat aside from the group
and quietly listened.

David brought them up to date and handed photos of the shooter
around to everyone. Joe was a wizard and had downloaded the
picture and made copies. David explained that he was positive that
this was Jake's shooter, the man who'd tried to run-down Cynthia,
and the man who'd shot him in Oregon.

At this point, Mrs. White stood and asked David for a copy of the
photo. She studied the picture before saying, "Such evil! How are we
to deal with such evil people!"

"I'll be perfectly honest. My first concern is Cynthia. She—and
all of us excepting you, Terry—are armed and can shoot thanks to
Mr. White. But, this man doesn't let you see him. He, and his boss,
think they are smarter than the rest of the world. They never give
warning. This man shoots when he thinks you'd least expect it. Just
as he did with Jake and me. Makes me even wonder if that letter is
worth it." He stopped and there was silence.

"I have little doubt that he knows we are here in this house at this moment. I think he'll be concealed somewhere out front in the dark. That's how he operates. He loves surprise and concealment. He'll want quick action simply because he'll be worried about that picture. I think we need to be very careful tonight. Can we get out the back and circle the block staying out of sight?"

Cynthia spoke. "David, I think you should let Bob and Dad go out. You don't look good."

"No. We need three out there."

Terry would remain with Mrs. White and Cynthia.

The three men made sure that no light showed as they opened the back door. They slipped out with Joe leading them through the large backyard and through into the street. They circled the estate and moved through trees and shrubs approaching the White residence from the front. They'd separated and were studying the street and all possible areas of concealment.

Bob first sighted the small figure in the parked car. It was well hidden in a dark spot. He slipped quietly up to the rear of the car and saw the barrel of a rifle barely sticking out of the driver's window.

Bob reached up and grabbed the barrel pulling sharply down. The butt flew up into the the shooter's right ear. It must have hurt like hell, Bob thought. But the shooter made no sound. Instead, his hand fumbled inside his jacket. He was trying to pull a semi-auto out just as the car door behind him flew open. He started to turn when he felt an arm circle his neck and a hand grab his wrist.

"Don't." David reached and slowly removed the handgun with his wounded shoulder hurting badly. It had been immediate and spontaneous.

It turned out that the shooter was a felon with two guns in his possession. So, he was locked up. *One down,* thought David. One to go.

CHAPTER 39

Empty Frame

CONRAD SATEROUS WAS RATTED ON. The very man he'd hired to kill for him ratted.

It was Frank who'd worked a deal. He proposed it to the DA who was glad for the opportunity. He badly wanted Saterous. And Winifred Powers, the weasel faced little killer, turned States' Evidence. Winifred had foolishly kept the rifle he'd used to shoot Jake. The bullet that wounded Jake was a match with the rifling of the gun he had outside the White residence. And, the gun was owned by Saterous. Winifred P. swore that Saterous had hired him to kill either Jake or Cynthia in order to bring David to his knees. It hadn't worked.

Conrad was found hiding in a dark cellar room in the basement of his large mansion. He was surrounded by a large variety of documents framed and hung in a dark room with just the right temperature. All the documents had been stolen. Most belonged to private parties, some to museums, and others to various public and private institutions. All were in excellent condition.

Saterous was admitted for life to an institution for the criminally insane. Before the week was out he committed suicide.

Frank called David and asked him to meet with him at Owen's office.

"Sure. Could I bring Cynthia, her Dad, Bob and Terry," David asked.

After hemming and hawing, Frank gave in and said OK.

David S. Leonard

At the meeting, Frank turned to David and said, "You'll get a kick out of this Dave. When we found Saterous he was sitting in a dark room with a flashlight . . . *a flashlight!*

There was no other light. He was looking at his stolen goods by flashlight. He was especially obsessed with *an empty frame . . ."* and Frank was shaking his head.

All David could think of was how Jake would laugh at hearing this. He'd be sure to take Jake a strawberry milkshake.

END

CPSIA information can be obtained at www.ICGtesting.com
Printed in the USA
BVOW032223281012

304158BV00001B/13/P